Secrets Off The Ice

Alexandria Miller

I've always said my first book will be dedicated to the real Mrs. Johnson,
who was the first teacher to read my writing and encourage it,
even when it only kind of fit the journal prompts.

1

Of course, Leo and I are the first ones at the rink. We practically always are, but especially this week. No one wants to be here at seven AM during Christmas break. We had a tournament the last few days and now we're right back at it. Apparently winning two out of three games during the tourney wasn't enough for Coach. We have to practice on our last real day of break. In three days, school is back in session.

Leo drops his bag on the floor of the locker room next to mine before he finally looks over at me. "Why are you so tired? You didn't even come over to Lev's place with us last night."

"Couldn't really sleep." Because there was someone tossing and turning in my bed all night. And then I got woken up at six this morning. "Might not want to let your dad hear anything about last night, though. At least, if the snaps I was getting are any hint." Leo vaguely waves me away with his hand. Now that I really look at him, his olive toned skin has a little more of a green undertone to it today. They must've really gone at it last night after we got back. I throw an arm around his shoulders and lead him out of the locker room.

"C'mon man, let's go stretch until everyone else gets here. Start getting whatever out of your system and wake you up."

When we reach the bottom of the stairs, we look at each other in unison. With a quick nod, we start running. Who needs to be awake to race up a set of stairs? I'm at least two stairs ahead of him. That hangover isn't doing him any favors. When I turn to look, ready to brag about my victory, the toe of my tennis shoe catches on the top concrete step. Before I can even think to catch myself, my knee slams into the corner or the stair and I'm flat on my stomach.

"I touched the top first. I still win," I claim, pushing myself to a sitting position and bringing my feet up.

"My feet touched the top first. Your face hit the top and that doesn't count."

"My face didn't hit...I don't think." Rubbing my face to check for any sore spots, my hand comes back with a distinct lack of blood. I tend to get a lot of bloody noses. If I hit my face, my nose would be bleeding right now. "Nope, we're good. The best looking person on this team is still intact."

"You're an ass," Leo laughs. Pulling up the left leg of my joggers, I find what's practically a bloody crack across the middle of my knee. "That's real pretty. Have fun washing the blood out of your pants."

I shrug, thinking about how much laundry I have waiting to be done at home already. "At least my pants are black. Harder to tell." Hopping to my feet, I bend and straighten my knee a few times. Doesn't seem injured, just sore.

"So what did you want to do?" Leo asks me. He may be the coach's son, but I'm the captain.

"I was thinking a few laps." Leo looks at me like I'm trying to kill him. "Dude, three laps is less than a half mile. You'll be fine. Though, I have a feeling your dad may add more laps when he sees how crappy most of the team is going to look."

He rolls his eyes at me, but nonetheless takes off his hat and lays it on the nearest table. He does the same with the softshell jacket he strips off, so he's just wearing a tshirt and sweatpants. Leaving my layers on, I start jogging. A lot of people walk or run on this balcony. It's not necessarily a track because it doesn't have lanes, but eight laps to a mile and it's open almost all the time as long as there aren't games. The only other one up here right now is a girl on the other side.

Along this top level, we circle the rink. When we're playing, this is a great place to watch and the air is crisp enough to wake you up in the morning and keep you from overheating. After one lap, Leo almost starts to look better, granted, the girl passed us as we began our second lap. Long sleeves and pants with her hair streaming behind her. At the end of the second lap, Leo drops to the floor looking like he's ready for a nap.

"One more. I said a few, not a couple."

"You're annoying," Leo says, forcing himself to his feet. Just as we start again, I feel something hit my back causing me to stumble. When I look up, the girl is running past us again. Did she seriously push me?

Looking to Leo, I gesture toward the girl and start to open my mouth. Before I can say anything, though, Leo says, "Maybe you should've moved when she told you to."

I didn't hear anything. "She could've hurt me!" I answer instead.

"You already hurt yourself today. Your face probably would've survived this one too," Leo laughs.

"Watch out or I'll make it four laps." I tell him before we silently jog the third lap. Looking straight ahead, I watch the girl in front of us. She has good running form. She's not skinny, but she must run a lot. She doesn't seem tired or like she's struggling. She must have headphones in because I can see the wires trailing from her ears to a pocket on the side of her leggings. I wonder what she's listening to. When we're done, Leo slumps onto the floor again.

"You have a whole practice ahead of you, buddy," I tell him, grabbing his hand to pull him to his feet. We take the short cut stairs back down to the locker room. There, most of the team has arrived. "Let's go warm up, boys," I say. I don't have to say it loudly with this comatose room. I count as they file past me. We're missing two.

Upstairs, Leo asks, "Why didn't you leave me up here if we were just coming back?"

"You would've fallen asleep," I answer cheekily. "Plus, you probably needed those extra stairs." Then, I call out to everyone, "Where are Hunter and Lev?"

"Did they die?" one boy asks. Great, they were bad enough last night that someone is questioning their livelihood.

"Has anyone heard from them this morning?" I try. Simultaneously, half the team takes phones out of their pockets. If they aren't awake yet, they will be after all the calls and texts they're going to get. That is, if their phones aren't dead. Once everyone is paying attention again, I turn and walk further onto the track. Halfway down the straightaway, I start doing lunges with a twist. On my fourth one, I hear a thunk behind me followed by laughter. When I turn around, I find Dave laying on the ground. Are they still drunk if they're tipping over, or just that hungover and sleep deprived? Ignoring them, I keep going. It'll only encourage them if they get attention.

After ten, I turn around with a line forming behind me as I wait for everyone. Next, I do high knees. Just before turning around again, I notice the girl from before running toward us and dodge to the side. I can't get a good look at her face since she's going the same direction as us, but she seems familiar. "Side!" I yell, trying to get her room to run. I don't need anyone else getting pushed, especially with how the guys are today. Only a few guys move over and she looks like she's doing an obstacle course between dodging everyone and the vending machine that we're near. Next is butt kickers. At least no one has issues with these ones that stay upright. Grapevine each way. I don't hear her, but out of the corner of my eye, I see her dodge past me again. Watching her, I notice she stops after that lap. Maybe she's done. After a length of soldier kicks, I lead everyone back down to the locker room to wait for Coach Fulton.

We barely sit down before Coach comes in, looking everyone up and down. He shakes his head at us. "Why is Hudson the only one who doesn't look like a zombie today? He was the top scorer this week. If anything, he should've been the one celebrating and not doing so well this morning." Oh, so he knows. "From now on, I'm instituting a new rule. I'm calling three of you every night at 9pm. If you don't answer and sound sober, you're not playing the next game. You won't know who's getting the call each night. Questions?" Silence. Actually, I might hear crickets. "That's what I thought. Hudson, take them for a mile."

Nodding, I head back upstairs again. If the groans behind me are any indication, no one is happy about this. Leo comes up alongside me and asks, "Can I just do five laps since I already did three?"

"No, because I did three too and have to run. You'll just be less hungover than everyone else," I answer curtly. If he's going to whine, he shouldn't have gone out last night.

Looking around, I assume the girl is gone. No sign of her up here. We start jogging. Halfway through the first lap, I notice movement on the ice. When I look, the girl is out there. Is that allowed? Isn't this our ice time? She's just skating in circles.

I try focusing on running, but my eyes keep being drawn to the movement below us. At one point, she's spinning in the middle. Eventually, she does a jump. Nothing fancy like you see in the Olympics, but a jump nonetheless.

On the fourth lap, Leo catches back up with me. If it hadn't been for the fact that I haven't lapped anyone, I'd almost think that there was no one behind me anymore. It's almost like everyone is mad at me for being semi-conscious when they're not with how far back they're staying. "Later, you want to grab some lunch and go snowboarding with some of the guys?"

Do I want to? Sure. Can I? Not so much. "I have to work pretty much right after practice."

"Well, we aren't going right away. People need more sleep."

"Well, I work until six tonight."

"How do they give you such a long shift on a Friday?"

I have to try really hard not to look at him like he's an idiot. "We don't have school today. That means I can work."

"Just ask your parents for money and don't work so much. Do what I do." He puts his hands behind his head as though he's relaxing, but falls behind without paying attention to the running.

"So, do nothing, get my parents to pay for everything, and then spend my free time drinking?"

He starts to nod, but pauses when he realizes how bad that sounds. "Whatever, man," he answers before dropping back again.

On our sixth lap, I see coach come out to the ice. When he sees the girl, he looks mad. Not a good day to get on coach's bad side. Even though I could probably understand him if I tried, I block it out. I wouldn't want to be on the receiving end, so I'm not listening.

After one last lap and everyone looks almost dead from running, we go put on our gear to start actual practice.

2

I barely make it to work in time, and I only work a half mile from the arena. I think Coach was trying to kill people. At one that afternoon, my watch goes off with a message from my mother. "What time do you work until?"

I have to roll my eyes. It's on the calendar at home, but god forbid she actually look at it. I simply type the single number into my watch and send it. In less than a minute, she responds again, "Can you come home early? We wanted to go out." Not sure whether to be weirded out by my parents being more worried about date night than my job, but at times they make me glad my room is upstairs and theirs is in the basement. I don't want to risk hearing anything I don't want to hear.

At 3pm, I get a text from Leo. "Dude, we're just getting to the ski hill! Come by when you're done with work!" Yeah. Right. My parents just made sure that wasn't going to happen.

I do manage to get enough work done that I'm able to leave at 4, though. When I walk in the front door of my split level house, it's eerily quiet. Is no one home?

Upstairs, I find my mother sitting on the couch in the living room. "Leo wanted me to go snowboarding with the guys tonight," I tell her.

"Regardless, you came home early like I asked, so you know you're not." She finally looks up from her book and gives me that mother look that tells me to stop while I'm ahead.

Nonetheless, I have to try once more. I sit down on the couch next to her and say, "Can't I just this once? Just for a couple hours?"

"No, you're lucky you can play hockey. You're not going out and doing another sport where you can potentially injure yourself. And we're going out so you need to watch Penny." I'm not getting out of this. Then she adds, "You could take her with." She knows I can't do that. Seeing the hesitation on my face, she says, "You know, your life would be a lot easier if you didn't keep her hidden away."

"It was your idea when I started at this school."

She pushes her short hair back from her face as she says, "I didn't think you'd ever tell anyone."

As if on cue, I hear a door down the hall open. We pause our conversation, and I hear a small voice yell, "Daddy!"

As I stand to look the direction of the voice, I see a small girl with brown hair streaming behind her flying towards me. I grab her under the arms, throw her up in the air, and catch her before giving her a hug. "Hey there, baby girl. What were you up to today?"

"I played doll house!" she answers excitedly.

Brushing my hands through her hair that's nearly the same color as mine, I tell her, "Sounds like we have a date night tonight." She leans backwards to look at me inquisitively, so I continue. "Grandma and grandpa are going on a date, so you're stuck with just me tonight. Think you can handle that?"

"Yes, daddy! We play!"

"We also need to eat and go to sleep. For dinner do you want mac and cheese? Or maybe grilled cheese?"

Wiggling out of my arms, she starts to head to the kitchen. Halfway there, she turns and crosses her arms. "Box or pot?"

"Which would you rather?" I turn the question back on her.

"Pot!"

"Instant Pot it is then. We better make sure we have all the ingredients, though." With that, she does a spin that's surprisingly graceful for an almost four-year-old and heads into the kitchen. Looking to my mother, I say, "Better get ready for your date. I guess Penny and I are starting our supper."

My mother simply nods her head before moving toward the basement. At the top of the stairs, she pauses. "Are you sure you two will be okay tonight?"

I sigh, "Mother, I've kept my daughter alive for more than three years. I think I can handle a night."

"You've kept her alive living in our house, using our food, and using us as babysitters so you can work and play hockey." With that, she does head downstairs.

3

"Dude, important question," Leo says as he comes up to me on Monday morning. I've been at my locker for less than 30 seconds and he already found me. I'm not ready for this.

After sleeping in all through Christmas break, Penny didn't want to get up to go to daycare. After I spent so much time fighting her to get ready, I didn't get to make any coffee. I was going to stop and get some at the gas station, but then drop off took longer than usual too. I wish I could just go home and sleep.

"What?" I ask shortly.

"Wow, maybe I don't want to ask you," Leo says, appearing offended.

"You're fine. Now, what's your question?"

"Taco Bell or Taco Johns?" Seriously?

I give him a deadpan look. That's the question? When it's barely eight in the morning? "Taco Johns, obviously. Potato Oles."

"Okay, I agree. McDonald's or Burger King?"

Another one? "McDonald's. Better fries."

"I'm not sure about that choice, but okay. Subway or Jimmy Johns?" Leo asks.

"Subway. More personalization options."

"But the bread at Jimmy Johns…" Leo's face looks like he's fantasizing about the bread.

I roll my eyes, grabbing my books for my first class. "Are we done now?"

"No, now championship rounds. Taco Johns or McDonald's?"

Closing my locker, I head down the hall lined with blue lockers to my homeroom with Leo on my heels. "Taco Johns. Better potato products."

"Now, last but not least…" He hesitates as though I don't know the options I have left. As we walk through the door into Mrs. Johnson's classroom, he grabs my arm to stop me. "Taco Johns or Subway?"

"They're so different, it depends on the day."

"No, they're not!" Leo is offended again. "They're both meat and veggies with carbs on either side."

"You can't argue that a taco is a type of sandwich."

"I definitely can. Especially a hard shell."

"You know what? If you can get half this class to agree that tacos are a type of sandwich, I'll buy you some before the game tonight. If half the class agrees with me, you're buying me a sub." I won't mention that tacos seem like a really bad idea before a game.

"You got a deal!" As I walk to my seat, Leo starts asking people. He asks Hunter and Jamie from our team, Liz, one of the quiet girls, and Aliyah, one of the ridiculously smart girls in our class. It's 50/50 so far with the girls and boys each split. I didn't think anyone would agree with him. Wait, how many people are in our class? Counting the desks that are usually filled, it's an even 18. What if it ends up totally even?

By the time the bell rings, everyone has wandered in – Leo quizzing each of them on their way to the seats. Lo and behold, it's actually even. Leo moves to his desk to my right and collapses into it dramatically, leaning back against the wall. "What now? I want my tacos."

"Maybe Mrs. Johnson would -" Another person walks in the door. A girl with long brown hair framing her face and wearing jeans and a baggy hoodie for a rock band. She doesn't go here. Or at least, she's new. She looks familiar, though. When I look to Leo, I know he doesn't know her either, but he's sitting on the edge of his seat, ready to add her to his survey. "Dude, don't scare the new girl," I tell him. She looks nervous enough as it is. She glances down to the paper in her hand before looking back up. As she walks up to Mrs. Johnson and introduces herself, our red-haired teacher nods emphatically. She gestures to the room, I assume telling her to sit down. There's two open spots. One right in front of Leo, the other in the back corner by the door. Surprising me, she sits in front of Leo. Front of the room. Miraculously, Leo doesn't survey her the second she sits down.

By the time attendance is called and I discover her name is Piper, Leo is practically vibrating in his seat. Mrs. Johnson tells us we can talk among ourselves for a minute. Without hesitation, Piper leans down to take out a book that she had put in the wire rack under her seat. When she sits up, Leo leans forward in his seat. "Hey, new girl." Her shoulders tense and she turns around warily.

"Yeah?" she says.

"Question for you," Leo answers. This is painful to watch. The new girl's eyes dart around, I'm sure trying to figure out how she can get out of the conversation. I watched people we know do it, so I can't blame her. She doesn't answer him, but she doesn't turn back around either, so he goes on. "Are tacos a sandwich?"

Her eyebrows wrinkle until a frown is formed. Then, she narrows her eyes at him and looks around, like we're trying to prank her. "No, they're not."

"Are you sure, though?" Leo tries. "It's meat, veggies, and condiments with carbs on the outside. That's basically a sandwich."

"I think the textbook definition specifically says bread, not carbs. I barely count wraps."

"You said barely!" Leo answers like he won. "A softshell taco is basically a wrap and you count a wrap."

Piper rolls her eyes at him. I like her. Sassy and exasperated by Leo. My kind of person. "Leo," I say to get his attention. "Give it up. I win. Tacos aren't a sandwich."

"But-"

"No. You owe me dinner rich boy." Pursing his lips and crossing his arms, Leo finally leans back in his seat.

When Piper looks between us, the corner of her mouth is turned up. I think she's trying not to laugh. Just then, Ashley joins us, sliding into my seat that barely fits me so that we're sitting in the same place.

"What's he pouting about?" Ashley asks, lifting her chin toward Leo.

"He lost a bet."

"Is that what the taco question was? Thank god. I thought he was losing it."

"Nope, you know how he is," I answer, looking up toward Piper. She turned around again and looks to be reading. "Can you sit somewhere else? This seat isn't big enough for two."

"I'll sit with Leo. He doesn't mind," she answers, walking around to slide into his seat. Actually, it looks like she sits more on his lap than in his seat.

"You may talk until the bell rings for you to go to your first class," Mrs. Johnson says, "But sit down please." Ashley doesn't move. "In a seat." Ashley slides off Leo's lap, but stays in his chair. "In a seat that someone else isn't also occupying." With that, she sticks out her bottom lip. She gets up to walk to her seat behind me, but pauses. When I look, I see that her seat has been taking over by someone else. When she crosses her arms, I know it won't be a good day. Ashley in a bad mood this early is obnoxious. Instead of starting something, though, she crosses to the other side of the room to talk to some of her other friends. Works for me.

4

Since I won the bet, Leo and I are going to Subway before the game. Not everyone likes to eat before games, but otherwise, I wouldn't get to eat until like 10 tonight. Talk about low blood sugar. Leo rides with me. Since his dad is the coach, Leo will ride home with him tonight. There's almost no one at Subway when we walk in. The only other customers are a couple eating at one of the tables. I suppose, not a lot of people are getting dinner yet at 4:30.

I pause a few feet from the counter to decide what I want. A girl comes from the back of the store, says, "I'll be right with you" over her shoulder, and starts washing her hands. Leo looks over to me and nods his head toward the counter to tell me to go. Shaking my head, I tell him, "You go first. I'm still deciding."

When he steps up, I notice that the girl working is the new girl from school today. She's the pretty one I've seen working before. I knew she looked familiar this morning, but I couldn't figure out why!

"What can I get you?" she asks him, probably just like she asks everyone else. He orders his meatball sub and, while it's toasting, she turns to me. "And you?"

"I'm actually going to get two subs tonight." Leo looks at me strangely so I tell him, "This way I can eat something after the game too."

"The game? What do you play?" the girl, Piper, asks.

"Hockey! Hudson here is one of the best guys on the team!" Leo says as he puts his hand on my shoulder. I think Leo is going for a wingman thing, but I don't need him to matchmake. I'm busy enough as it is. "You should come by, Varsity is at 7!" With that, the toaster beeps and she turns to pull Leo's sub out. Before she can say anything else, Leo looks at me and says, "I know I'm supposed to buy your sub, but I'm not buying two."

When she turns to set his sub back on the counter, she has a thoughtful look on her face and answers, "I might, but I work until after the game starts." Then, turning to me she asks, "So what are these subs you're getting?"

"So, a footlong and a six inch both wheat bread. The footlong I'm going to do steak with mozzarella cheese – toasted. The six inch, just a turkey with american cheese – not toasted." With a small nod of her head, Piper starts making the subs. When she turns around to put my steak sub in the toaster I realize something else. That brown ponytail. "You're the one who was running and pushed me the other day!" When she turns around to finish putting the turkey on the six inch sub, her cheeks look a little pink, but her visor is blocking most of her face when she's looking down. She has a braid along the side of her head pulling into the pony tail.

"Well, maybe you should pay more attention for other people running," she answers with surprising snark. Then she adds under her breath, "Or at least move when I say move." She seems like the type of person who would be too shy to be that snarky.

"I didn't even hear you. Are you sure you said it out loud?" Wait, does that sound mean? I don't want her to think I'm an ass.

"Yes, I'm sure. I heard myself say it over my music." Looking to Leo, she asks, "Any veggies on here?" When I look to Leo, he's looking between the two of us, despite her waiting expectantly.

"Dude. Veggies," I say to focus him.

"Ah, no. Parmesan and oregano. That's it," he says quickly, probably realizing how weird he was being.

My sub comes out of the toaster, and Leo's gets wrapped up before she looks at me again. "Veggies on yours?"

"Steak gets lettuce, tomatoes, pickles, cucumbers, and barbecue sauce." I pause while she piles on the veggies. When she looks up at me, done with that one, I go on to the next. "Turkey gets lettuce, tomatoes, pickles, and mayo." Once that's done, she wraps both of those up too.

"Are you guys paying together or separate?"

"Wait, you don't think – no. Even if I was gay, he is not my type," Leo quickly corrects.

"Or you mentioned that you're supposed to buy my sub?" I say to make him realize he's being an idiot. "I mean, if it weren't for that comment and me having other things to pay for, I almost would've bought that sub for you even though you won the bet. Now you're not getting anything from me." I sigh and shake my head at Leo. "Not your type."

Leo simply rolls his eyes and says, "Let's make it a meal. I'm going to grab a bottle of Gatorade."

"Chips or cookies?"

"As much as those doughy chocolate chip cookies tempt me, I'm going to go with the chips." She taps the computer screen a few times before telling him the total. He swipes his card and then it's my turn.

"I'll do one meal with chips and a Gatorade as well. And let's add a couple of cookies too."

"You know you can get three cookies as like a deal, right?"

"I guess I'm getting three cookies then. Two chocolate chip and one of those raspberry cheesecake ones. So, you'll stop by the game?" I ask, trying to catch her eye. What color are her eyes? The visor on her head is shading them too much.

"Maybe if you can try to score for me?" Finally, she really looks at me. Brown eyes. With a half-smile on her face, I can't help but smile either. But crap, Penny is promised my first goal of every game. I have to figure out my excuse to go pick her up without Leo and get her this sub for dinner.

"My first goal is already promised, but I'll try to get a second one for you."

Her smile drops from her face as she hits a final button on the computer and tells me my total. Pulling my wallet from my back pocket, I pull out my debit card and swipe it through the machine.

After we grab our Gatorades and chips, Leo stops at a table. When he starts unwrapping his sub, I ask, "What are you doing? We usually eat at the rink."

"I don't want to forget to put the chips on the sub. Otherwise, I'll eat the chips before we get there." When he layers enough on the meatballs for his satisfaction, he wraps it up and heads for the door. "So, what's with you and the new girl?"

"Nothing? We just met today. You've seen every interaction we've had." I speed up my steps to get to my truck. When I climb in the driver's seat, I set the subs in the middle and pause, faux realizing something. Without a word, I climb out of the truck. Pulling my hockey bag from the bed of the truck, I unzip it, pretend to rummage around in it, zip it back up, and put it back in the bed. Slamming the door shut, I walk back to my door and climb into the cab where Leo is waiting.

"What was that?" Leo asks me, munching on the chips he didn't add to his sub.

"I forgot to pack my lucky socks. I'll drop you off at the rink to start eating, but then I need to go home and get them."

"I'm not letting you play without them with the way you've been playing lately, so no problem." With that, I shift into reverse and pull out.

5

I didn't just go home and come right back. I had to pick up Penny from daycare, go home to get warmer clothes on her, we ate, and then we came back. By the time we get there, Leo must be done eating and in the locker room. Most of the guys are probably already in the locker room. I walk Penny through the front door, bag over my shoulder. She has her backpack on and is carrying my hockey stick for me. Her season pass is in my wallet, so I have to fish it out to show the woman selling tickets. She's one of the guy's moms, but like most other adults, they just assume she's my sister. I mean, we'd have the same last name that way too.

Once we get past the ticket window, I kneel down to be face to face with her. "Okay, if you need anything, Grandpa is working the penalty box. Got it?" She nods and pushes my stick toward me. "We gonna high five tonight?"

"Yes!"

"Well I guess I better score then, huh?"

"Course!" she answers with so much enthusiasm it has to be obvious.

Apparently tonight I need to score two goals after seeing Piper earlier. With that, I kiss the top of Penny's head and lead her through the doors and into the rink. She heads up the ramp to find somewhere to sit while I head under the stands to the locker room.

I have to walk about halfway down the length of the rink before I get to our locker room. When I open the door, I walk into silence. As I step through, I see why. Coach was already talking the team before we go warm up. I'm later than I thought.

"Dude, where were you?" Leo calls.

"I couldn't find my socks. I got them, though."

"Well, get those socks on your feet because you need to be out in 2 minutes, Melville," Coach says. With that, I give a nod and start dressing. As Coach Fulton tells us to get out, I finish dressing with the light blue and white jersey. Finally, I pick up the light blue helmet and put it on my head. I push through the guys to the front of the line. First out to the ice since I'm captain. As I wait for Coach to open the door and for the announcers to call us out, I take a deep breath in through my nose. The smell of the ice is just what I needed to focus in. I stand up straight to my full 6'3" and throw my shoulders back. I'm ready.

It's only a few minutes into the first period when I get my first penalty against Forest River and it's a five minute major off the bat. Nothing like just about half the period being done by the time I get out. I know why they made boarding a major now, but it's still annoying. Unfortunately, that means the team plays shorthanded until I'm out. The other downside is that it's five minutes spent in the penalty box with my father since he's working the game tonight. Then, Penny proceeds to run over to say hi which makes my father look at me like I'm completely irresponsible. It's not like I can be responsible for her while I'm playing and mother didn't want to come tonight. It's not the first game I've let her run unsupervised, but I guess this early in the game – and with my father here – she just wanted to run over here. I tell her to go back to her seat with her backpack and, as I'm talking to her, Forest River scores.

"Dammit." I say, stomping my foot. I need to get out of here soon. My father clears his throat and when I look to him, he's looking at Penny. She's giving me wide eyes and I realize what I said. "Sorry baby, bad word. You go back to your seat, or I can't find you when I score."

"Oh yeah!" she exclaims before starting to run back around the rink.

"Five, four..." my father starts to warn me to be ready. I stand, he opens the door, and I am back on the ice.

Leo's heading down the ice. I race down and hit my stick on the ice. There's two guys coming toward him. "Here. Pass!" I yell. He passes it to me. I shoot.

"Top cheese!" He yells skating toward me. And I'm surrounded. Leo tends to be our playmaker. He doesn't always score, but he can almost always get it to someone who can. As the guys back off, I find Penny in her normal place behind the team's bench. She's jumping up and down. We skate by the bench to get high fives and once again, I'm in front. This time, because I scored. With that, it's time for a line change so I jump the wall and sit on the bench. Behind me, there's kids going crazy. I turn around, find Penny in amongst all the little kids, and put my hand up against the glass so we can high five. Then, back to watching the game. Waiting for my turn to go back in.

When I score again in the second period, I remember the conversation earlier. Is she here? Looking up to the stands, I first scan the student section. She's not there. Then, as I look towards the middle where Penny is, I find Piper sitting practically right next to her. Wait, what? Piper is smiling and looking towards me, so I point toward her. She's not wearing her work uniform anymore – just jeans and a light blue sweatshirt. Her hair is still in a ponytail, but the visor is gone. But why is she by Penny? And Penny is talking to her. I know she's not shy, but she doesn't usually just start talking to people.

"Hudson. Snap out of it," Leo says, grabbing my shoulder and shaking it. "I know you like the new girl, but we have a game to play." As I skate off the ice, I question myself. I like the new girl? Do I? I haven't had a crush on anyone in, well, a little more than four years. I haven't had time to. No, I don't have a crush on her. I just met her today. Basically. I turn to look at her behind me once I'm sitting down. She's talking to Penny still. It has to be a weird coincidence, right?

By the time I look up nearing the end of the third period, Penny is fast asleep...with her head on Piper's lap. What the actual...?

Finally, the game ends. We won 3-1. I try to dawdle in getting undressed because not only do I hope Piper leaves before I get out there, but I want the rest of the rink to clear out. Especially when sleepy, I can't trust Penny not to call me dad. I hate that I have to take these precautions, but I've gone through way too much work the last two and a half years at this school for people to find out now. I run my bag and hockey stick out to the truck before I get Penny. If she's asleep and I have to carry her, I don't want to be carrying all my gear too. Finally, I head back in to get her. Maybe father took her home. That could make it easier.

Alas, when I get out to the rink, I look up to find Penny fast asleep on the stands. She's hugging her doll and using Piper as a pillow still. Piper, to her credit, is just leaning against the level behind her and reading a book. Before I approach, I watch them. Piper is reading The Great Gatsby for English class. She's in all but two of my classes – physics and psych. Piper and Penny have matching braids on the right sides of their heads. That's actually kinda cute. There's a Dr. Pepper and bag of twizzlers next to Piper that are nearly gone. When I mount the stairs and approach, Piper looks up. I don't know that she was wearing makeup earlier, but she is now.

"You came," I start.

"I did. This little one found me and asked for a braid. Do you know who she belongs to? No one has come for her yet." I can't tell if she's suggesting something, or if she's asking totally innocently. The way she's asking me almost sounds accusatory.

"Umm, well," I push my long hair back out of my face before rubbing my neck. "I'm the one taking her."

"Oh, your sister?" Do I lie? If Leo is right, do I be honest?

Rather than answering, I sit on my heels in front of them and touch

Penny's arm. Practically as soon as her eyes crack open, she murmurs, "Daddy."

With that, Piper's eyes widen. "Oh." She doesn't say anything else. Maybe she wasn't suspecting anything.

"Yeah, no one really knows. They assume the same thing you did, and I just don't correct. Anyone. I've never corrected anyone." Piper nods as though she understands, but I can see in her face that she doesn't. I throw the loop of Penny's backpack over my shoulder, then, tucking my hands under Penny's armpits, I lift her. She must be tired because rather than wrapping her legs around me like a monkey, she stays limp and I have to support her. She's getting too big for this. I feel like I need to explain a little more. I don't want Piper to think badly of us. "We didn't have the easiest time at my last school, so we switched and kept things quiet."

"We?"

"Well, Penny and I. I know she doesn't go to school yet, but it was a big change for me. After that first year, that is." When she tilts her head, asking without asking, I add, "I stayed home for the first full school year. Just about her whole first year." Why am I talking so much? She probably doesn't care. She doesn't need to know these things. For all I know, she's going to go around telling everyone at school tomorrow.

Piper follows me down the stairs and toward the door but doesn't say anything. Finally, at the outside door, I stop and turn back to Piper. "Please keep this quiet. We're getting so close to being done and I don't want to ruin things now."

Piper tucks a light pink hat on her head and says, "Of course. Thank you for inviting me. And getting the goal. I think I understand now why I couldn't have the first goal." And she walks away. With that, I bring Penny to the truck to get home for bed.

*****

When I get home, Penny is fast asleep in her carseat. I unbuckle her and pull her arms out of the straps, throw a backpack strap over my arm, and pick her up. I'll make a second trip for the hockey bag in the back of my truck.

Without knowing, they found each other. Apparently, Piper made an impression. Penny may not be shy, but she doesn't usually get her hair done and fall asleep on strangers' laps. To add to that, the fact that Piper was letting her sleep while she read. She didn't seem too concerned about the strange child who was all alone.

Did she know before I told her? She didn't seem all that surprised when I said she's my daughter. I mean she reacted, but maybe she suspected and was waiting for confirmation? Walking to the door, my foot starts to slide on a slippery spot on the sidewalk. I move my hand to protect Penny's head in case I fall while I move my foot, looking for dry ground. I do, but that happens to be hitting my foot against the single step up to the door. Penny lifts up her head, looking around to figure out what woke her. Shushing her, I open the front door of my house, slip off my black dress shoes, and put them on the mat in the corner. There's a scuff on the right one from that step. I'm going to have to clean it off before the next game.

I go up the stairs to the main floor of my split-level house and turn left down the hall. When I get into her room, I lay her down in her bed. I sneak her shoes off first; can't have any dirt or food she stepped on in the bleachers getting in the blankets. In a drawer under her bed, I find a set of pajamas with Paw Patrol on them. She wakes up just enough to help get them on before she snuggles back into bed, requesting a blanket. Of course, she's laying on them, so I find a spare I keep in the top of her closet for this reason and spread it on top of her.

Creeping out of her room, I head back down the hall and to the front door. I put tennis shoes on to have a little more grip. Just inside our front door – behind the door when it opens – we have a plastic canister of ice melt for just this reason. Little patches of ice that we don't need to break the whole spreader out for. I take it out with me, finding the shiny spot on the sidewalk that almost made me lose my grip in those shoes, and sprinkle a handful of crystals on it. I don't want that to happen again, especially when I'm carrying Penny.

I leave the canister on the step while I head to my truck. I shut the passenger door I had left open and pull my bag up over my tailgate. Tossing it on my shoulder, I head back to the house, grabbing the ice melt to return it to its home behind the door on my way. Taking my shoes off when I get inside, I bring my bag down to the laundry room. Letting everything air out as soon as possible at least decreases the smell that accumulates.

I head back up the stairs and when I turn the corner on the landing, flipping the lock on the front door, I see someone standing at the top of the stairs, startling me. Looking again, it's just Penny, having woken up and come to find me.

"I have bedtime snack?" her small voice asks from the top of the stairs. She rubs an eye with her hand and goes back to standing eerily still, watching me from the top of the stairs.

"It has to be something healthy. I saw what you were eating during the game." She and Piper were sharing twizzlers. I shake my finger at her and smile, making sure she knows she isn't actually in trouble. She jumps up and down in excitement twice before seeming to remember herself and where we are. She stands still as a statue, as though waiting to see if she'll get yelled at. When she doesn't, she quietly walks into the kitchen. My parents probably aren't asleep yet, but there's a good chance that they're at least sitting in bed reading.

Penny goes to the kitchen bar and scrambles up onto the high stool so she can watch me in the kitchen. Tonight, we're keeping it real simple. I take a clementine from the fruit basket and start peeling the skin. "You're not even going to get me a bowl tonight?" Usually, she's more helpful. We try to keep her bowls, plates, and cups within her reach just for that reason.

"Sowwy daddy. I tired." She puts her elbows on the counter in front of her and leans forward.

"Make sure you watch those elbows when grandma and grandpa are around," I say, reaching to grab at her elbows on the counter. She quickly takes them away, apologizing.

I take a Mickey bowl from a lower cupboard, setting it on the counter in front of my daughter. Somehow, she already has the beginnings of bed head even though she was only in her bed for a few minutes. I pull apart the first couple slices and put them in the bowl. Her tiny hand instantly reaches in to swipe one, smiling as she takes a bite. "Tank you, Daddy."

"You're welcome," I answer, finishing pulling the clementine apart for her before washing the sticky juice off my hands.

As she eats, I try to smooth her hair down, finding the braid that's still half there and deciding to leave it. It'll probably come out on its own overnight. "Did you have fun at the game tonight?" She doesn't come to every game, so it was a bit of a treat for her.

She nods her head enthusiastically. "I like her. I got candy!"

"I know you did. Did you like that kind of candy?" She nods again, taking another bite of an orange slice. "Would you like to see Piper again?"

"Yes, yes, yes!"

Do I want her to keep seeing Piper? Would Piper be one to stick around if I do keep talking to her? I don't want Penny to find someone new she likes and then never see her again.

"Okay, we'll see, Monkey. Finish your snack so you can brush your teeth before bed." Penny nods her assent and eats the last slice without getting too distracted. When she's done, she gets off the chair – pushing it in, and brings the bowl to drop in the sink. When she reaches the sink, she stands on her tiptoes to just get the bowl over the edge of the counter before it clatters down into the sink. From there, she heads straight for the bathroom between our rooms. She washes her hands and brushes her teeth while I put the bowl in the dishwasher and make sure the counter is clean before bed.

I change into some flannel pajama pants to sleep in and find her sifting through her books, looking for the perfect one. "Only one tonight." When I don't give in to the puppy dog eyes or pouty lip, she agrees. She takes one from the top, handing it to me before crawling into bed and under her blankets.

Penny waves me over that she's ready. When she moves, the braid falls in her face, reminding her it's there. "Look, pretty hair!"

"It is pretty. Should daddy learn how to do that?"

"You can't."

"Why not?" I'm a little offended.

She merely shrugs. "Read?"

"What do you say?"

"Peas?"

Laughing, I lean back against her pillows and put my feet up to read Where the Wild Things Are.

6

When I wake up on Tuesday morning, I find myself in Penny's bed. She's still asleep next to me, but she usually wakes up when I try to get up. Checking my phone, I find that my alarm didn't go off. Or I didn't set it.

I push the hair out of Penny's face and almost feel bad that I have to wake her up, but we only have 45 minutes before I need to be at school. Before then, we both need to get ready, and I need to drop her off at daycare.

"Hey, Monkey," I whisper. When she doesn't react, I shake her shoulder gently. "Penny, it's time to get up and get ready for daycare."

"I don't wanna. I sleepy," she whines as she rubs her eyes.

"Daddy is going to get in the shower. You need to find clothes and brush your teeth." Hopefully my not even acknowledging her tiredness is the answer.

Luck be in my favor, when I get out of the shower, she's just coming into the bathroom. We both brush our teeth and I throw her hair into a quick ponytail. I'm sure it's not going to make her any happier, but we don't have the time to decide on a hairstyle and do it. While I put my jeans and boxers on, I let Penny pick out my shirt. Then, with a package of poptarts to go, we put on our jackets, grab our backpacks, and head out to my truck.

It may be a historically fast drop off with her walking in while I carry her carseat for my mother to use when she picks her up. I can never pick Penny up on practice days. Checking the time as I jump back in the truck, I realize I don't have time for coffee or to pick up a real breakfast on my way, so I head straight to school. When I pull up to the parking lot, I must be one of the last people to arrive. There are cars double and triple parked, but I manage to find a spot where I'm only the second in the row. This is ridiculous. This is what happens when you tell a bunch of teenagers to park in a lot where you can't see the lines due to ice and snow.

The bell rings to go to class and I start running for the door. I have to go to my locker and get to the classroom. It's not far to go from my locker, but three minutes to get from the parking lot to class might be too much. Shuffle steps inside to hopefully dry off my shoes enough that I don't fall on my ass trying not to be late. Coach makes us do killers if we have any tardies.

Instead of taking time at my locker, I go right past it. I can bring my backpack to homeroom. Once there, I collapse into my seat and take a deep breath right as the late bell rings. I made it.

"What's wrong with you this morning?" Leo asks.

"I forgot to set my alarm. I woke up 45 minutes ago." Tipping my head back to look up, I silently thank God I didn't get caught speeding or injure myself or anyone trying to get here in time.

"It's a miracle if I have that much time. Why do you look so stressed?" he asks. With that, I have to look over at him.

"How?"

"I shower at night after games or practice, so I don't need to shower in the morning." He shrugs as if that's the only thing that takes time in the morning. I suppose, for him, it just about might be the only thing.

Finally, I look over at Piper. She's looking down at The Great Gatsby as though she's reading, but I get the feeling she isn't. She's listening to us.

When out of nowhere Leo asks me if cereal is a type of soup, she gives herself away. She snorts. Two days in a row with his weird food questions. I don't blame her for laughing, but she obviously doesn't want to talk to me if she's pretending to read. Maybe I scared her away last night after all. I just really hope she doesn't tell anyone.

By the end of the day, Piper hasn't said one word to me. She must not like me after all. It doesn't matter if I do like her or if I'm willing to have her in our lives. She'd talk to me if she liked me. For all I know, she never actually liked me. I mean, we only knew each other for a day. At the most, she maybe thought I was cute. No one can develop a crush that fast. Right? So that means I don't have a crush on her either.

7

We're going to have a picnic. Maci and Penny are holding hands, walking in front of me. They're trying to decide on the perfect spot. I forgot how much Penny looks like her. Maci's brown hair falls down her back in perfect beach waves. Penny's will do the same thing fresh out of the bath, but I can't seem to get them to stay after I brush her hair in the morning. They're walking the same too. Penny does have my eyes, though. When we reach a flat area of the park, Maci bends down and whispers in Penny's ear. Waves of hair cover her face so I can't see it. I haven't seen her face since just after Penny was born. Penny runs off to run up and down the hill nearby.

Maci unfolds the blanket she had been carrying in her other hand. It's a big blanket, big enough for us all to sit on. With a good grip on the blanket and her back to the wind, she throws it up into the air to let it spread. When she brings it down to the ground, it's perfect.

I bring the picnic basket over and plop it right in the middle of the blanket. I wonder what she packed.

When she sits down, I collapse next to her. I'm so much taller than her that I just about feel like a giant trying to fold my limbs under me. I don't think she's gotten taller since I last saw her. When she giggles, it sounds different than I remember. Leaning over, I kiss her cheek, but something isn't right. Then, she turns toward me and I see brown eyes looking at me. This isn't Maci, this is Piper. I'm somehow glad it's Piper, and yet I knew it all along. Did something change, because now she looks right? Curvier and taller than just a minute ago. Her face isn't as sharp as Maci's, but the hair is still similar. Have I seen Piper's hair down? Wait, it was down at school that first day. Now I'm not sure if it's that similar.

Piper has makeup on like at the game she came to. She's gorgeous. Opening the picnic basket, I find three sandwiches, a big bag of Doritos, and some homemade cupcakes. She's so good to us, making us food to go for a picnic. Us. Where's Penny? When I look up, I catch a glimpse of her running down with her dress flowing behind her. She always has to test if a dress spins enough, so it doesn't surprise me that it flows behind her either. As she's running straight down the hill, she's coming right for us. Her hair is blowing in the wind and she reaches out her arms. She's older and her hair is longer than it should be. When she reaches the blanket, she collapses right into Piper's lap, hugging her. Piper wraps her arms around Penny and grins as she hugs her back. Then I see something shiny. There's a ring on Piper's finger. Holy crap. I look down at my hand and there's a black one on my finger.

"Hey, daddy," I look up to the voice that is definitely my daughter, but not quite.

"Yeah, baby girl?"

"Thank you for mommy."

I feel like I give myself whiplash when I sit up. I actually slept in my bed last night and Penny isn't in here. What time is it? When I look toward the clock on the bedside table, I put my head in my hands. 5:28.

My alarm is going to go off in two minutes. With a flop, I fall back into bed. Then, holding my hand up in the air, I make sure there isn't a ring on my finger. I feel it with my other hand. Nothing. Okay, good. I'm not ready for that. Now, I guess I better get going. Maybe I can get through the shower before Penny wakes up.

I almost do. As I'm wrapping my towel around my waist in the steamy bathroom, I hear the doorknob turn and the door flies open, nearly hitting me. In the doorway, I find Penny with her hair in every which direction looking at me. "I gotta potty," she tells me.

With that, I open the door wider and step around her to my room. I just manage to get my boxers and a pair of jeans on before I hear myself being called. When I enter the bathroom, she's brushing her teeth. Her hands keep reaching up to push her hair out of her way, but it isn't working. With a laugh, I reach out and collect her hair to get it out of the way while she finishes brushing. Once she spits, she rinses the tooth brush before putting it in the holder on the counter.

"Should we fix this mess up?" she nods, so I pull out the detangler and brush. I wonder if that little braid last night made it better than it would've been. Nothing can stop her hair from being a mess by morning.

With a little hop, I can tell she wants to sit on the counter so I pick her up and let her sit cross-legged there, facing the mirror. Detangler. Spray. Spray. Spray. Brush through. As I'm brushing, I look between Penny and I with our matching opalite blue eyes. By the time I'm done brushing, she doesn't have the waves anymore. I frown, what do I need to do to make them stay?

"Daddy, don't be sad." I look up at the little voice. She's watching me in the mirror.

"I'm not sad, baby. What hair style do you want?"

"Like yesterday?"

"The pony I did?" she shakes her head. "You want a braid like Piper did on Monday?" she nods now. Crap. "I don't know how to do that. Daddy will learn soon, though. Okay?"

She nods again, but this time, more subdued. We decide on pigtails and separate her hair in half. While I'm brushing her hair into a pigtail, I notice her watching me, curiously. I look up to myself in the mirror, and I think I know why. I'm smiling.

"You happy, Daddy?" she asks as I brush the second pigtail into place. I don't know that anything happened that made me happy. I had that weird dream last night, but it definitely wasn't real. Maybe I had another dream that made me feel more upbeat this morning. I needed it after yesterday morning.

"Like a Phoenix rising from the ashes, baby," I answer, giving her a kiss when I lift her off the counter. I love her so much. Sometimes I wish things didn't happen the way they did, because I could probably be a better father. If things happened differently, though, I wouldn't have this perfect little girl.

She giggles and pokes the tattoo on the left side of my ribcage. "Phoenix from ashes," she answers. In today's case, the ashes is yesterday's exhaustion. I lead her back to her room to find clothes and remind myself that I need to go find a shirt. Do I wear a hoodie, or maybe look nicer? Wait, why do I need to look nice? It isn't a game day. When I tell Penny to find me a shirt while I make her cereal, she comes out with one for me. She didn't pick out a button down, luckily, but a plain black, long-sleeved Henley. That works.

*****

Pulling into the school parking lot after dropping Penny off at daycare, I find myself thinking about that dream again. We were both wearing rings. I assume that meant we were married. And I thought she was Maci at first. I think I was glad she wasn't Maci. Why would I have a dream like that about someone I just met? Was Leo right? Is this what happens when you have a crush on someone?

A big bump in a pothole shakes me out of that mental spot and I nearly faceplate. Of course this is what happens when you like someone. Not what I needed right now.

Another big pothole bump. I need to pay more attention or I'm going to get stuck just pulling into the school parking lot. At least she already knows about Penny... Wait, she knows about Penny. I really hope she doesn't tell anyone.

I park the car and swing my backpack over my shoulder as I just about jog to get inside. I need to know if people know. Can I transfer this late in the year if they do? I mean, I guess Piper just did it, so I probably could. Do I need to just because of her, or only if she tells? That'd mess up my last season of hockey. I don't think I'd do that just to get away from some girl, but maybe. I guess it depends how people react.

Walking through the door, I run my hands through my hair. It's just about down to my chin now. It wasn't worth keeping up anymore. Took too much time and money to get it cut all the time. When I push it back now, it stays pretty well so it doesn't get in my eyes all the time. I wasn't sure coach would let me keep it this long, but he isn't a stickler. Plus, I'm on my way to the all hockey hair team if we can get to state this year. You don't actually get anything from it, but it's kinda cool to be named.

When I arrive, Leo is just walking the other way down the hall. "Meet me in Wood's room," I get yelled at me as he walks away. I'm not sure why we always go there in the morning when our homeroom is with Johnson. The only time we're in Wood's room is for study hall at the end of the day.

I drop off my backpack before heading to find Leo. I barely step through the door before Leo takes one look at me and asks, "What happened after the game?"

"What do you mean? I went home and went to bed." I'm not lying, just omitting everything Penny related.

"You're smiling," he answers similarly to how Penny did this morning. I look at myself in a window and realize I am. Why does that keep happening?

"I just had a weird dream last night." Also not lying.

"Did it involve the new girl?"

"She has a name."

"Fine, did it involve Piper?"

"She may have been in it." I almost regret telling him that. Then, a second later, I do regret it. He raises his eyebrows at me a couple times before putting his hands on the desk he's sitting on top of and making a thrusting motion.

"No!" I exclaim. "That wasn't it."

Before I can say anything else, he yells, "Hey, McMillan!"

"Who-" I start to ask as I turn around. When I see Piper walking past the door, I look back at Leo. "I'll see you in class," I tell him before running after Piper. Now he's going to think I was lying and it was a wet dream. I'm not sure if the real answer is worse or not.

"You're not going to tell anyone, right?" I ask as I match her speed.

"What?" she looks over at me before saying, "Who would I tell? You're just about the only one who's talked to me."

"But you wouldn't tell anyone?" I ask, trying to look into her eyes as she stops at a locker.

"I said last night I wouldn't." She sounds like she's getting impatient with me already. Probably not a great sign for that dream coming true.

"Can you teach me how to do a braid? She asked me this morning and I had to say no." Piper rolls her eyes and looks over at me again. When I give her the puppy dog eyes, she sighs.

"I can try, but no guarantees you'll get it." I nod as she grabs her books. I follow her all the way to our homeroom. Inside the door, she pauses. "Where did I sit the other day? There were people in here yesterday morning to clue me in," she whispers to me. I'm not sure why she's whispering since we're the only ones in here.

Walking across the room, I pat the desk she sat in. Then, in a split decision that's sure to get me some comments from Leo, I decide to take his seat behind her. He can sit in my spot. It's closer to Ashley anyways.

8

During homeroom, Piper starts trying to teach me to braid. For the most part, all I can tell about what she's doing is twisting her hair around each other. It's hard to focus on how to braid, when I just keep watching her face. She doesn't look like she's concentrating, she looks calm. Somehow, she looks more calm than I've ever seen her. Usually, her foot is tapping or she's fidgeting, but as she braids her hair, she looks relaxed. How her hair doesn't end up knotted, I don't understand. When she finishes a strand, she drops it before separating another chunk of hair from the rest on the side of her head. When she hands it to me, I freeze. I separate it into three even-ish sections. Then what? I don't even remember how to start. Moving one piece from the right to the left, then the left all the way to the right, I'm sure I'm doing it wrong. I drop her hair and sit back. "I can't do this," I say, crossing my arms.

With a laugh, Piper simply turns around to face forward, then says over her shoulder, "You can try again later." As she turns, she runs her fingers through her hair to untangle what I just did. She undoes her own braid with a little more work. Then, pushing all her hair back onto my desk, she leans back and starts at the front of her head. She isn't doing a little braid in the middle like she was showing me or a big braid down the middle like I see a lot of girls on the girls team do. She starts at one side of the front, and keeps pulling more hair into it. How is she not forgetting what to grab and what she just let go of? She's nearing the back of her head. Is she somehow going to go all the way around her head?

"You're in my spot," Leo says, coming up to me. With that, I'm wrenched away from watching Piper braid.

"I thought you'd like my spot better anyways," I answer. As I turn to look toward my usual seat, Ashley walks past it and sits right behind it. He follows my gaze, and simply nods before going around the front of the row to reach my usual seat. Now will he let me get away with this more days, or is this a one day thing?

*****

We don't talk much the first couple of hours. To be fair, that doesn't mean anything with her. Mr. Dunn just doesn't allow talking in his class. He's the type that will give an instant detention if he so much as sees a phone. Sometimes he even does it if we're suppose to be working and he hears a whisper. You better hope you're not the one someone is whispering to, either, because you also get the detention. I can't afford a detention. Not when I need to get to practice after school.

Second period, I would've tried to talk to her. We sit right by each other - me, in the front spot against the wall where she sits in homeroom with her right behind me. Today, though, Mrs. Johnson decided we need to do research. It's hard to talk in secret when everyone is silently doing research on our chromebooks. We have to research colleges. Something to do with another assignment she plans to give us in the next couple of months.

I'm sure a lot of people have done all the research. Some of them have even applied to colleges by now. Maybe they've been accepted too. I've barely looked. I mean, I've been getting scouted for a few years. Sophomore year after I started back up in hockey, and school, I had a couple big names come talk to me. University of Minnesota and Bemidji. Junior year, those same ones plus some further away like North Dakota and a couple in Michigan. This year, though, not so much. The big schools have already filled their rosters for next year with people who were willing to make commitments early on. Penny was an infant. I could barely make the commitment to high school hockey. Even if I wanted to try to walk on, I wouldn't get a scholarship so I'm not sure I could afford it. I still don't know that I'd be able to manage Penny and going to college, but at least she'll be in preschool next year so it's a little more feasible.

I start to search local schools. I may not be able to go far away, but that doesn't negate all good or even decent teams. The first one I search, one that hasn't talked to me at all, but isn't out of the question being a smaller school, has a very obvious button for me to push. "Scout me." With that, I fill in my information. The next school, I can't find anything about scouting. There's vague mention of hockey camps coming into the season where you can try out, but I guess if they don't hear about you other ways, they don't want you. I could potentially email the coach since I've talked to him before, but that seems unprofessional. Maybe Coach could email or call them. That seems more logical.

Looking up to the board, I read what she wants us to research about schools. Majors, extracurriculars, tuition, and if there's on-campus housing. Guess I need to figure out what I want to do rather than just picking a school for hockey.

As we are leaving College Writing, Piper looks to me and asks, "Can I ask you a question?"

"You just did," I say, trying not to smile.

"Did Penny really ask you to braid her hair?"

"She did, but we don't talk about her with this many people around," I answer, trying to give her a meaningful look.

"Hasn't anyone else done it before? Like Ashley?" I feel my eyes widen at that. Not just because she kept talking about Penny in the middle of the hall, but at the thought of Penny meeting Ashley.

"You think I'd let them meet?" I ask, shaking my head.

"But you guys-" she stops without finishing the sentence.

"Didn't I make it clear about absolutely no one knowing?"

She pauses at a door, must be her next class. Her eyes widen. "I guess," she says quietly before ducking through the doorway. I head one classroom further to Chemistry with Ms. Lamb.

The rest of the day goes without any excitement, and with minimal intrusive questions, until the last period. The last period of my day is a free period back with Ms. Lamb. I'm just trying to see what homework from the day I can get done when I look up out the window and realize it's snowing. Like, a lot.

Before I think about what I'm doing, I walk up to Ms. Lamb's desk. She gives me a look of surprise when she sees me next to her. "What can I do for you Hudson?"

"Can I go outside and start cleaning off my car? I don't have much time to get to practice after school so if I can save some time when driving will take longer-"

When I pause to take a breath, she simply says, "Go ahead. You better actually come back and not leave early, though." Nodding, I head outside. There's a door to go out to the parking lot nearly next to this classroom.

First, my truck like I said. On the floor of my passenger seat, I have a good scraper. One of those extendable ones with the brush that lets me push like a broom rather than just a brush going along half the length of the handle. These are much more effective for this wet snow that's coming down. It also has a squeegee which can be nice sometimes.

It doesn't take me long to push the snow off my windshield and headlights. Now, which car is Piper's? I should be able to guess. It isn't like a bunch of kids just started here or started driving to school since Christmas break started, so the lineup of cars hasn't changed all that much. I turn in a full circle, examining every car I can see while my feet crunch in the snow. I imagine it's the same sound my feet would make if I was walking in a world full of marshmallows. Other than the sounds of my feet in the snow, the world is so quiet with giant snowflakes falling around me.

Then, after I've made nearly a full circle, a light green Subaru catches my eye. I hadn't noticed that one before. I bet that's it. First, I'll just clean off the side windows. Make it discreet while I try to decide if it's hers. Luckily for me, she made it easy without realizing it. There's a Subway shirt in the back seat. It must be hers. With that, I decide I'm just going to clean the whole thing. Each window only takes two sweeps of the squeegee, though I do make sure I brush off the car doors too since so much piles on the handles when you clean the windows. I notice while cleaning her car that she has an old style, blue iPod in the cupholder and hooked to an aux cord. I can't imagine how old that is. Why doesn't she just connect her phone to her car with bluetooth?

With a shrug, I clean off the side mirrors. Easy to miss. Then, the windshield. That takes a little more work with how heavy the show is, but it helps that her car is short, kind of like her. Part of me wants to leave the hood and roof of her car, but I find it so obnoxious when people drive with piles of snow on top of their car. If it melts and refreezes, when it flies off it could hurt someone. By the time I'm done, there's even bigger piles of snow surrounding her car on all sides than there was before. She'll have a step in the deep snow to get in now. So, I step around in front of her door. At least pack a little down for her, though, now I have snow in my sneakers. Her car is practically clear other than the snow still falling and, with only five minutes until school is done for the day, I toss the brush back in my car and jog to the door to get in. I promised Ms. Lamb I wouldn't leave, so I should show back up and at least get the homework I was working on before it's time to go.

The bell rings right as I walk through the door into the classroom. Dodging my classmates, I get my homework off my desk in the back of the classroom and head for the door. I need to find Piper to see her reaction to her car.

Surprisingly enough, I find her at her locker still. She isn't quite in the senior hallway. She's down a side hallway just past ours, and ours is already kind of a side hallway. Nonetheless, her locker is on my direct route outside from my locker. She's rooting around for something at the bottom of her locker, adding things to her backpack.

"Can I walk you out?" I ask, leaning on a locker next to hers.

She jumps, before glaring up at me. Jeez, what did I do? "I guess, but it kind of seemed like you didn't want to talk to me." Oh, that.

"I want to talk to you. Just not about, you know, in front of other people. That's how secrets become not-secrets."

"Not-secrets," she repeats, rolling her eyes.

"Exactly. I didn't exactly tell people when she was going to come into existence, but it's amazing how fast things spread in the halls of a school."

Piper looks around, as if these are the halls I'm referring to. "Not here, my old school. I transferred. That isn't a secret."

"But why is," she says as if she's answering her own question.

"I was being bullied. Which isn't a lie," I answer with a shrug. Then, more quietly I add, "It just may not be the whole truth." A look of realization comes over her face and, before she can stop herself, she gives me a look of pity. "Nope," I say simply. After a questioning look, I add, "We're not doing that look. I've gotten that one too much. I'm going to the parking lot, and you're walking with me."

Rather than arguing, like I expect her to, she simply stands and pulls the zipper on the plain black, canvas backpack shut before throwing it over her shoulder. I close the locker door for her and we head for the door. "So, what's your plans for tonight?" I ask, seeing if I can change the subject.

"Work, eat, sleep," she answers simply with a shrug. "Same as last night."

"Do you ever not work?" I ask her. Partially curious, but partially concerned. How does she get homework done?

"I get two days off after today. Then I work through the weekend." She stops as though that's all she has to say, then adds, "Two days off in a row, though!" She looks close to celebration, and I smile. I wonder how she spends her days off.

When I turn around to look at her, I see she stopped, looking at her car. She frowns a little, before walking over to it. "You're not the one who cleaned it off?" I ask, faking surprise.

She gives me a confused look before saying, "No, I was in band. Someone else did it. It wasn't you?" She caught on that fast?

"Ummm…" Why do I feel like my face is on fire? It's too cold for my face to be this warm. I know it's below freezing if it's snowing, but I suppose it has to be warm enough to snow.

"No one else here talks to me. It had to have been you."

"I don't know, maybe you have a secret admirer." Why did I say that? Now she's going to think I like her. And I don't, right? I have a kid to think about. I can't like anyone.

"Maybe," she answers, giving me a curious look. "I do need to go to work now, though."

"Me too," I answer, trying to save myself. "Well, not work, but practice." Shut up now, Hudson, please. I point at my truck and say, "So, I'm gonna go. I'll see you tomorrow."

As I'm reaching for my door handle, I feel something hit my back. Turning around, I find Piper standing by her car laughing. When I try to reach the spot on my back, I realize it was a snowball thrown at me. I give her an accusatory look. She simply laughs again and says, "Bye, weirdo."

9

When I get home from practice, I simply drop my hockey gear on the landing just inside the door. I untie my black tennis shoes, take them off, and set them on the shoe rack that's pushed up against the wall. Then, I bound up the stairs, taking two at a time, without making a noise. You get really good at not making noise in this house, even while doing things that aren't supposed to be quiet. At the top of the stairs, I head straight into the kitchen. Mother, father, and Penny are all already sitting around the table with their plates made. I'm late and they're waiting for me. Dinner is served at 6 o'clock and it's 6:10 so they've been sitting there like robots for 10 minutes. Penny is fidgeting and I can tell she's sitting on her hands to keep herself from forgetting and eating – it's a trick I taught her from my childhood.

I quickly glance at the monthly calendar on the fridge, seeing that dinner tonight is beef tips with mashed potatoes. Tomorrow is spaghetti and I'm in charge of dropping Penny off at daycare, mother is picking her up. I'll have to talk to her about that.

There's a plate near the stove for me, so I dish up my food and slide into my chair across from Penny. "I'm sorry," I say quickly before I get a disapproving look. Too late. Already getting that look from mother.

"Let's pray," my mother says, as though it's an answer to me.

"Bless us, oh lord, and these thy gifts, which we are about to received, from thy bounty, through Christ our Lord. Amen," we chorus in unison. Then, unexpectedly, mother adds, "Lord, please help Hudson to practice timeliness. Help him to learn his priorities are his family and assist him in acting on things that will do him good."

Wow, I see how it is. I'm usually on time, but the one time I'm not, she calls me out. Literally to God. And what's this about things that will do me good and prioritizing? Is she still doing this about hockey, when my last season is almost over?

"Amen," my parents both finish. I'm not saying Amen to that.

"So anyways," I say, clearing my throat. My mother gives me a sharp look. We don't talk during dinner, but I need to discuss how tomorrow is going to work. "Do you have any appointments scheduled tomorrow morning?"

With a taken aback look, my mom answers, "Not until nine, why?"

"Would you be able to trade pick up and drop off with me?"

"How will you do pick up with practice?"

"We got switched to morning practice, so I can do pick up, but I can't get her ready and to daycare before school." With a nod, she says, "You get pick up after school. I can go in a little late." With that, we continue silently eating. My parents say that you shouldn't talk when you're eating because then you're distracted from the signals your body is sending you about when you're full. It's the same reason we've never been allowed electronics at the table.

If I don't have practice, and dinner tomorrow is spaghetti, I wonder… "Mother, may I ask you a question?" When she looks up at me, I can see it in her face. Not only is she annoyed at me for talking, but she suspects something.

Nearly laughing, my father answers, "You just did. Did you have another question?" He doesn't talk much, especially when it's a conversation that my mom can manage and thinks she needs to keep control of. Sometimes I question them being together. My father actually has a sense of humor sometimes, my mother is all serious all the time.

"I actually did. I was wondering if I could invite someone over for dinner tomorrow night."

They look between each other. Unlike most parents, they don't sit on opposite ends of the table, my father sits on one short end and my mother sits on a long end. I sit on the other end across from my dad, with Penny facing my mom, her back to the window. She gets distracted from eating if she sees animals in the backyard.

"One of your hockey buddies?" my father asks. Because who else would it be?

"Actually, no," I hesitate to say more, but I know I won't get any agreement without telling them who. "It's a girl."

"Are you sure?" mother asks, looking pointedly at Penny, who is scooping up mashed potatoes with her fork.

"She's actually already met Penny." My mother nearly drops her fork, but manages to make it look like she set it down on purpose. She takes the cloth napkin off her lap and wipes her mouth before she looks at me.

"You told someone?" I can't tell if she's glad I finally told someone, or if she's angry. It was only a few days ago that she told me it'd make my life easier if I didn't keep her hidden.

"I didn't so much intend to tell her. She was at my game the other day and Penny-" The little blue-eyed girl looks up to me with mention of her name, "fell asleep on her lap." Looking to Penny I say, "Do you remember Piper?"

She goes from swaying side to side as she eats, to bouncing with my words. "She did my hair!" I nod agreement when my mother looks back to me.

"She did a braid in her hair, and started trying to teach me so I can do them too."

"Well, if Penelope likes her and she's still being nice to you after that, I suppose she can come over tomorrow." Holy crap, I wasn't expecting it to be that easy. I mean, the last girl to come over that I'm not related to was Maci. The last time happened to be when Maci and her parents came over to discuss the pregnancy. "Have you told any of your hockey friends if you're telling people now?"

"Once again, I'm not telling people. I couldn't keep it hidden when I had to take a sleeping child off her lap in a nearly empty arena."

"You don't have to bring her to your games."

"I'm not going to take away the option for her to see me play hockey while it's an option since I'm probably not playing after this year."

"Of course you're not. You graduate this year."

"There's still college," I say, hesitantly. I've never brought this up in front of them.

"You can't go to college. You definitely can't play hockey in college. Too much travel. You need to work when you finish school."

"I've been scouted. I could go to college and maybe even have scholarships."

"And will those scholarships pay for you to have a nanny too?"

There's no use arguing with her. Obviously the answer to that is a no. With how she's reacting, it's obvious that grandparents babysitting are not the solution. I don't know what would be the solution, but it'd be nice if my parents thought the best of me when I haven't even tried yet.

*****

The next day when I get to school, I'm almost tempted to go find a chair to nap in in the library. I had to get up way too early for practice. Instead, I find the area where Piper's locker was. I don't remember which number it was, but it was somewhere in this area. I open all the ones without locks and find them all empty. I guess that leaves a total of two options. Therefore, I sit on the floor between them, lean my head back against the locker behind me, and close my eyes. I have plenty of time before most people driving themselves will get here.

Only a few minutes later, I jump awake to my shoe being kicked. When I open my eyes, Piper is smiling down at me from her locker, the one to my left. "Good morning, sleeping beauty."

"I just closed my eyes, definitely wasn't sleeping." When I pull my phone out of my front pocket, I learn I may have been lying. I've been asleep for at least 20 minutes just sitting here in the hall. "Okay, maybe I was sleeping."

Piper closes her locker door and sits down next to me. "No sleep last night?"

"No, I slept just fine. Had to get up way too early for practice." Reaching up to touch my hair, I push it back with my fingers. Totally dry already.

"Oh, I thought maybe Penny didn't sleep well or something," she drops her voice when she says her name. "She slept well once she fell asleep. Unfortunately, that means I need to stay in her room long enough for her to fall asleep and not wake up when I get out of her bed."

"Can I ask you a few questions?"

"Potentially," I answer hesitantly, eyeing all the other students walking down this hallway on the way to their lockers this morning.

"Why do you talk to me so much? You don't even know me." She sounds, I don't even know, annoyed maybe. She isn't looking at me, just looking down at her hands in her lap while her hair falls around her face like curtains.

"Do you not want me to talk to you?"

"No, I mean, I do want you to, but not just to be some fun fling that you're going to ignore in a couple weeks."

"What are you talking about?"

Then, she looks up at me. "You don't know anything about me. How would you know you want anything to do with me that makes me worth talking to?"

"I know you're beautiful, and you must like hockey at least a little. You run and you're good at braiding." I drop my voice and lean closer before adding, "You're good with my daughter."

If we were having a different conversation right now, I would think she's looking at my lips, maybe wanting me to kiss her, but then she says, "Don't say I'm beautiful if you don't mean it. You're just flirting to flirt. I'm sure Penny's mom was way prettier than me. I don't think you can have a kid that cute with just one person's genetics."

"So you think I'm good looking?" I ask in an attempt to relieve some tension. When she rolls her eyes at me and starts to get up, I say, "No, stop. Piper. I'm sorry. I don't mean that. Yes, she was pretty. You're prettier, though."

She pauses, still obviously not ready to take the compliment. "I promise I'm not just messing with you. You can ask anyone around here, I haven't dated since I started here three years ago. I'm pretty sure some people are starting to question if I'm secretly gay."

When I get a half smile from the girl kneeling next to me, I have to call it a win. "I have a feeling you're not, though?"

"Well, I can't say I've never seen a guy I thought was good looking, but I definitely tend to lean towards girls." I reach out my hand for hers and add, "More specifically, you. For a while, like, I try to pick Subway on game days specifically because you tend to be working, even before I knew you."

Piper's cheeks turn red and she stands up. She didn't take my hand. I don't know what she's thinking. Instead of answering, she says "It's almost time for class. You should get your things." So, I stand up and head to my locker.

*****

We don't get to talk much for most of the morning. She's focusing on reading The Great Gatsby, trying to catch up to where we're at in class. In Accounting, we have a test. I hear the teacher tell her she's exempt from it, but she still gets a copy of it so she can make sure she knows how to do it.

This is a fairly easy test, at least in my opinion. There's a list of transactions and dates and we need to make sure the ledger is filled out correctly. Pretty similar to what we've been doing all year, but she always adds whatever was on our most recent unit.

By the time I finish mine, I see that Piper's is pushed to the corner of her desk in front of me. She isn't paying attention anymore, she's just turned sideways in the L of the computer desk and reading her book again. Double checking my name is on top, I stand, grabbing Piper's on my way past, and set it on the teacher's podium in the front of the room. We're the first ones done. When I turn back around, Piper is watching me. The way she's staring me, with just a hint of a smile on her lips, I start to question if I spilled on myself during lunch or if there's food on my face. I push my hair back out of my face and look right back at her as I head for my desk. You can't have chemistry like this with someone you've never even kissed, right? I'm just imagining things. Or, maybe

I'm imagining her side of things. Personally, I'm glad I'm wearing jeans today and I only have to readjust a little bit once I'm sitting down.

When she turns sideways in her chair again, looking back to her book, I lean forward and whisper, "Are you cold or something?"

She turns to me, looking confused. "What?"

I touch her bare arm. She took off her sweatshirt at the beginning of class. "You have goosebumps."

Maybe I shouldn't touch her. At all. That gave me a weird feeling in my stomach. After a few seconds, I remember that it's just butterflies. A body's reaction to feeling nervous and, often, liking someone.

"I didn't realize I was so cold, but apparently I am," she answers me, still looking down at my hand that touched her arm. She reaches behind her to grab her sweatshirt and yank it over her head.

"Can you teach me braiding again?" I ask, hopeful that it'll get her to talk to me.

"I suppose," she answers after a few seconds hesitation. Then, she closes her book and turns her chair to face me.

*****

After school, Piper asks, "What did you do to my poor hair?" as she looks in the mirror inside of her locker, trying to untie her hair.

"I was braiding it!" I answer indignantly. I really was trying. I got further this time, after she went slower in showing me what to do. I thought I had it, but at some point something went wrong.

"Well, it appears you knotted it and I didn't have time to fix it during band. It's a good thing I don't work tonight so I can go home and try to get it out." She starts packing her backpack to go, rather than messing with her hair anymore.

"Can I walk you out?" I ask, pulling my backpack onto my shoulder.

"I guess," Piper asks more than says. Outside, on top of the windshield of her car, I left a pack of twizzlers and a bottle of Dr. Pepper. A whole pack of twizzlers seemed like a lot for an afternoon that doesn't have a hockey game, but it's all I know that she for sure likes.

"Where did those come from?" she asks aloud, pausing near her car to pick them up.

"You obviously have a secret admirer," I try.

"You did it. Again."

"I may have, but partially to apologize about kind of being an ass yesterday…and maybe a little bit this morning. Also, partially, to try to sweeten you up a little?"

She looks me up and down like it's going to be obvious what I'm going to say. Instead of torturing her, I decide to just ask. "Do you want to come over for dinner?"

"I'm not going to surprise your parents with an extra person at dinner tonight, and I didn't actually say I forgive you."

"You wouldn't be surprising them, they agreed last night."

She still hesitates. She swings one booted foot back and forth in the snow like she's thinking. "I want to know more about you, especially if I'm going to agree to meeting your parents. Like, what happened to Penny's mom? Where is she? Why do you have sole custody of her? Do you have sole custody or does she visit or have partial time? I know nothing about you other than Penelope existing."

I rub a hand across my face, and then bring in back to rub the back of my neck. That's a lot of questions, especially for a parking lot with people around. "I will tell you that stuff eventually. I need time. You have to remember. I don't tell anyone any of this. I can't tell you anything at school or people are going to overhear eventually. I don't know what to tell and what not to. I don't know how to explain any of it. Mostly though, I don't want to scare you away."

"I'm trying not to be scared away. It's a lot though. You have a kid. You're so much more experienced than I am. I've only had one boyfriend before and he dumped me. At homecoming. Because he got a hotel room for us and I wouldn't go up with him. So, he went up there with another girl. A blonde cheerleader. An Ashley, if you will." I can't help but cringe a little. That's horrible.

"I really do want to try. I just, like I said. When I haven't done this with anyone, the getting close thing, it's hard to remember how to do it." I shrug. I realize it probably isn't enough of an apology, but it'll have to be good enough.

"My parents really are prepared for you to come. Plus, Penny would love to see you again. She'll probably ask you to do her hair, though."

"I think I could probably manage to do her hair for you," she answers with a small smile.

"Not for me. I can kind of braid now. You just saw.. She'll just beg you because that's the main thing she remembers about you."

"Well, I'm not sure I'd count that braid, so I'd suggest you wait to try

it on her. But, maybe I'll do something fancy that you can't do yet."
When she sticks her tongue out at me, I laugh. She's okay.

"Should I pick you up for dinner?"

"How about you just give me your address and give me a time and I'll
drive there."

I don't know if she's an early person, on time, or late. I better give her
a time to ensure she's there early enough. "Oh, ummm, yeah, that
works. Be there at 5:30 or so. I don't have practice today so I just need to
do daycare pick up, but no point in being too early. Give me your
number and I'll text you the address."

"Oh, asking for my number now, huh?" I practically sputter for a
second before finally managing a yes. Why wouldn't I ask for her
number if she's coming for dinner? We exchange numbers – me texting
her my address.

"Before you go," I say as she's about to open her car door.

"Yeah?" she looks around like she dropped something. Between her
backpack on her shoulders and the twizzlers and pop in her hands, her
hands are full, but still.

"Can I give you a hug?"

"Oh, I guess, if you want?" I do want. I want to know what it feels like
to have her in my arms, even if it's platonic. She walks over to me and I
put out my arms, wrapping them around her shoulders and pulling her
close. She simply wraps her arms around my torso, and, after a few
seconds, I feel her relax into the hug, leaning her face against my chest. I
knew I'd like her hugs, and I hope she likes mine.

As soon as she starts to loosen her arms from around me, I let go, not wanting to hold her longer than she feels comfortable. "I'll see you later," I tell her, heading for my truck.

I swear I just barely hear her say bye before she slips into her car.

10

I'm pacing in the living room, waiting for Piper to get here. Penny is playing with dolls in her room, my father is making dinner, and my mother is reading a book in the chair behind me. It's only 5:25, and I know I told her 5:30, but I'm getting impatient. I already set the table with the cutlery we'll need and put cups at each spot. The plates are by the stove so people can serve onto them. Trying not to be too dramatic, but also probably not succeeding, I lay on the floor. I can't pace if I'm laying on the floor. Instead, I try to focus up at the Christmas tree that's still up. I stare up through the real branches at all the white lights. Right now it's just set normal, but sometimes we change it so they all flicker. Mostly, I change it so they flicker. On nights that Penny has a nightmare, it's nice to come sit out here in the dark, rock in the chair, and watch the lights, or, in the case of how I'm laying right now, it's fun to watch them flicker.

"Someone just pulled up outside," my father says, looking out the window from the kitchen doorway.

I try to sit up too fast and get caught in the lower branches of the tree. I didn't realize I was so far under it and now, naturally, my mom is glaring at me. Great start to the night. Looking out the bay window, I wait almost a full minute, and the car outside is still on. Isn't she going to come inside? "I'll go get her," I say, going down the stairs to slide my shoes on. If mom sees my tennis shoes on my feet with the back of the shoe bent under my heel, she might actually kill me, and she definitely will never buy me a pair of shoes again.

Piper parked on the side of the road in front of the house, straight out from the front door. With how deep the snow is, I have to follow the sidewalk over to the driveway, then jog down the driveway. It's a chilly evening, something like 10 degrees, and I didn't put my jacket on.

Reaching her car, I grab the door handle and open her door. "Why didn't you park in the driveway? Or come in?"

"Because I was hoping you'd come out?" She answers as though it's a question.

"And the real answer?"

"I'm scared to meet your parents? I'm not good with people."

"They're not scary, or at least not too bad. They're a bit formal, though, and I totally forgot to tell them to be normal." With that, she gives a small laugh. I sit on my heels just inside her car door. I can feel the heat pouring out and, if anything, she might come inside if she gets cold. "Plus, you're great with Penny. I told them that and that's what got them agree to having you come over.

"All I do is braid her hair and she falls asleep on me. That's not that hard."

"Exactly, not that hard. So you can come in," I answer, standing up and offering my hand. She ignores my hand as she shuts off her car, but still doesn't move. "The spaghetti is almost done and dinner is at six. We need to get inside soon or we'll be late."

"Spaghetti?" she asks.

"Yeah, I figure it's a basic meal that most people would be agreeable to."

"You're not wrong, I guess we could probably head in then." There's a small smile on her face. Is she flirting with me?

"If I said there's also cheesy garlic bread?" I ask. It may not be proper, but I want to know Piper's reaction to good food and get an idea of what she likes. She obviously isn't against carbs if she likes spaghetti, but I feel like cheesy garlic bread is a whole step further.

"I'd say we actually should go in." I hold out my hand again, and this time she takes it as she stands up out of her car. I pull her close, but realize that this would probably not be the most opportune time for a first kiss. Plus, I look over her head at the house. My father is watching out the window. Yeah, definitely don't want him watching our first kiss.

I close her car door for her when she moves out of the way, and, my hand still wrapping hers up, lead her to the door. When I open the front door, she asks, "We're just going to walk in?"

"I mean, I could knock if you want, but I feel like that would be more strange when I live here." I can't help but smile at her. She's so nervous, but also so cute. Now that I have her in the light, I can see she's wearing gray leggings with a plain black, long sleeve shirt. Unfortunately, the shirt is too long that I can't see how her butt looks in the leggings. "Come on in, take off your shoes," I say, using my hand at the small of her back to guide her in.

When I take off my shoes, I make sure to fix the backs of them so my mother won't notice I put them on wrong. She slips off her black boots she had been wearing earlier, and stares down at her socks. "You're looking at your socks like they murdered someone," I point out.

"I meant to change into white socks. Something plain." When I look again, I notice she's right. The socks don't even match. One is blue and one is yellow.

"They're the same movie, at least," I tell her, trying to cheer her up a little. "They're cute and I don't think my parents will care." When she looks pointedly at my feet, I add, "I only own plain white or plain black socks. There's not much mixing and matching you can do with that." I honestly don't know that I'd wear funky socks with cartoon characters, let alone not have them match, but that's nothing against her.

"Should I just take them off? Stuff them in my boots?"

"No, you're fine. We don't want your feet getting cold. Now they're probably listening to us, so we should stop dawdling. Reaching for her hand as I go up the first couple stairs, I miss and grab her wrist. When she pulls her wrist out of my grasp, I go back down. I take her hand and lace my fingers between yours. I wouldn't have thought her small hand would feel so right folded in mine, but I don't want to let it go now. When I head up the stairs this time, she follows.

At the top of the stairs, we turn right into the living room. "Whoa," she whispers, staring at the tree. "How long do you guys keep it up? I could see it from outside."

I love that where we set up our tree, you can see it shining through the bay window from the road. "Second Sunday in January we take it down. This weekend after our last Christmas celebration is over."

"Don't you want to keep it up forever?" She asks, wonder in her voice as she moves closer to the tree.

"Well, by summer I feel like there wouldn't be any pine needles left on it," I joke. She probably figured it was a fake tree since mom vacuumed today. When I look under the tree, I realize that's probably why I got glared at. Now there's a bunch of pine needles on the ground again. Oops.

Next thing I know, I'm being pushed out of the way. Penny realized Piper is here. She runs over, somehow never making a noise on this carpeted floor, and wraps her arms around Piper's legs. Piper looks down to see a small head pressed against her leg. She reaches down and runs a hand through her brown hair, saying, "Hi there, little miss Penny."

"You came!" the high-pitched little munchkin voice says.

"I did. Did your daddy tell you I was coming?" Penny nods her head as well as she can while staying fully attached to Piper. It's so weird to hear someone else refer to me as her dad, let alone be so casual about it.

"Hey monkey," I say, trying to catch Penny's attention. When she doesn't respond, I take a hand that's wrapped around Piper's leg. I tug a little on her arm and say, "Come here so Piper can meet grandma and grandpa." When Penny lets go, she holds onto my hand as she comes to me, putting her arms up for me to pick her up. I put my hands under her armpits and toss her in the air. She's giggling as I catch her to have her sit on my hip.

Piper spins around, as though she forgot there were people for her to meet. When she finds my parents, mother standing practically right next to me and father being in the kitchen doorway, she says, "Mr. And Mrs. Melville, it's so nice to meet you. Thank you for letting me come for dinner so last minute – I tried to tell Hudson I didn't want to be an inconvenience in you having to figure an extra person for dinner, but he wouldn't take no for an answer." She says it so fast, I'm amazed I could understand it all. From there, she hesitates. I can see her questioning what else she should say since no one has answered her.

Surprising even me, my mother steps forward to give Piper a hug. "It's nice to meet you dear." She releases her quickly and, as I watch them, I try to figure out what Piper sees when she looks at her. Brown hair, speckled with gray. She's wearing glasses and she has the same blue eyes as Penny and I do. "But please, call me Beth. My husband here is Patrick."

I look back to my father when my mother says his name. His head is clean shaven. Overall, I look more like him, though his nose is crooked now from getting in fights in high school and college. My father has wide shoulders and looks like someone that definitely played football at some point. The biggest thing that makes it so he doesn't look intimidating is his brown eyes. Somehow they soften his whole face.

"It's nice to meet you two," Piper starts, and then cringes, realizing she repeated herself. "So, umm, what do you two do for work?" That's the first question she comes up with? It's not bad, but it's a random one, at least, I think so until I look around our house and realize, depending how she grew up, maybe our house looks nice.

"I'm a lawyer," my father says. "And my wife here, is in finance." And with the uninteresting conversation, Penny wiggles until I set her feet back on the floor. Once her feet are touching, she runs down the hall toward her room. "Are you a senior this year as well?"

"I am, yes," Piper nods. It seems like simply knowing the answer to that question is boosting her self esteem.

"What is it you're interested in doing next year? Our son, his older brother," my mother uses a hand to refer to me as not being the one they're talking about. Pretty familiar. "is getting ready to go to medical school next year." They have to brag about the one they can since they're pretty convinced I've ruined my entire life.

"Oh, I'm not sure yet," Piper starts so I jump in to save her.

"She's in all the high level courses. Calc, college writing, physics. Plus, she wasn't even here for the accounting unit that we just took the test on and she aced the test." Her face reddens with my praise.

Conveniently, Penny reappears holding a book. She tugs at Piper's hand until she looks down and asks, "Read book?" I can see in my mother's face what she's thinking, so I try to put on my best warning tone and say her name. Quickly, she puts the book behind her back and comes over to lean against my leg. She doesn't like getting in trouble. "I sorry, Daddy. Adults talking."

"No, sweetie, come here," Piper says. "I'll read you a book." Piper squats down in front of Penny before asking, "What one did you pick out?" Hesitantly, Penny shows her the book. The Velveteen Rabbit. "That one was my favorite when I was your age!" Piper tells her.

When Piper looks around for where to go to read, Penny points at the window before running over to stand there. "Read here." So, following directions, Piper picks Penny up onto the cushion in the window before settling herself in. As soon as Piper picks her feet up to pull them into their window seat, Penny exclaims, "Belle!"

Pipers face goes a little pink again. I think she was hoping no one would notice, but now Penny pointed out the socks to everyone. "She's my favorite princess. What about you?"

"Yes! We read book!" So with that, they start reading. My parents watch them for a moment longer before both heading into the kitchen to finish up dinner, leaving me standing in the middle of the room like an idiot. I can't tell what my parents think of her, but I can tell that now they're whispering in the kitchen. I guess I'll just sit on the couch while they read.

"Do you have a stuffy you sleep with?" Piper asks Penny when they get to the part about the little boy needing the bunny to go to sleep. When Penny shakes her head, Piper says, "Really? I had a doll that I brought with me everywhere. One time, I forgot her when I went to my grandma's house so my mom had to come get me!"

Penny giggles before saying, "I don't need stuffies. Daddy sleeps in my bed!" She covers her mouth and giggles even harder when she looks over at me.

My face is getting warm as Piper says in the most appalled voice, "Your daddy falls asleep in your bed?" Okay, my face might be getting more than just warm.

I'm not sure how I expected to get through this night without her learning more about me, but the fact that I sleep in my toddler's bed was definitely not what I was intending. "After hockey practice, how could I not fall asleep reading Goodnight Moon or The Rainbow Fish?" I shrug, trying to seem nonchalant. Piper spends a few moments looking around the room, taking it in. I notice her looking at our formal dining table, the one we don't usually use. The one we haven't used since, well, probably in a little more than 4 years.

When she spends too much time looking around, Penny pokes her leg and says, "Read!"

She laughs, before continuing from the book, "The little Rabbit was very happy after that." Quickly, Penny leans back into Piper, settling in like they're meant to be together. Is this what Penny is missing out on with not having a mom in the picture?

It can't have been more than a couple minutes when suddenly, a small body lands directly on my lap. I try to blink away the sleep that washed over me and catch her so she won't roll off and onto the floor. "You sound like a piggy, Daddy!" Penny claims, pushing a finger against my nose. So, naturally, I make some pig noises at her. As she starts giggling, I lower her to the floor and tickle her.

When I hear more laughing, I look up to find Piper sitting on the floor by the recliner, watching us. "What do you think you're laughing at, Missy?" I ask her.

"Ummm, nothing?" she answers, trying to school her face.

"Oh, really now? I don't think I believe that. I think you're laughing about something."

"I don't think so," she says, shaking her head. I'm on my hands and knees, crawling towards her now. She starts backing away trying to go toward the kitchen, but she falls backwards into the recliner. I see her look for Penny, but she's holding on tight to my foot, holding on and trying to keep me from getting to her. When Piper laughs again when I'm only a foot away, I smile. I like seeing her when she isn't being serious. She's so serious at school, but she's actually being silly with us now.

Then, I reach her and am tickling her. I'm laughing too and I can't breathe. "Penny, help me!" she calls when she gets a breath in. Penny tries to jump in and starts tickling me under my armpits. When that doesn't work, she moves to my sides where she's most ticklish and it doesn't do anything. "Get his feet!" Piper guesses.

When Penny goes for my feet, I have to back away for a second before diving toward her again, attempting to tickle her again. Before I get close enough, Piper quickly stands up, scoops up Penny in her arms, and I hear her whisper, "Where's your room?"

Penny wiggles out of Piper's arms, grabs her hand, and pulls her down the hall to her room. When they're both inside, one of them slams the door shut.

As I go past the kitchen, my mother says, "You guys need to settle down. Dinner is nearly ready."

I nod at her so she knows I heard her and, when I reach the door, I knock lightly and call, "Little pig, little pig, let me in."

"She has no idea what you're referencing, you know," Piper calls back.

"Seriously? I'm a horrible father." I like being able to be who I am with her.

"Evidently!" she calls back, laughing.

"Hairs on my chinny, chin, chin!" Penny calls back confidently through the door.

Okay, that's it. That's great. I laugh and my forehead falls to hit the door. I hear Piper start laughing too and she opens the door a crack. I pick up my head and grin at Piper before saying, "I'd say that was probably too many words."

"No kidding," she answers, rolling her eyes. "Did you want to come in? You're only allowed if you pinky swear you won't tickle anymore. Otherwise, I'm not responsible for any potential injuries."

"Ouch."

"Which is exactly what you'll be saying if you tickle me."

"Fine, I'll pinky swear when I get in."

I watch through the crack as she picks up Penny and opens the door the rest of the way. Getting inside, I hold out my right pinky immediately as a truce. "No tickling."

She answers with her pinky and as I wrap my pinky around hers, I start to lean forward before pausing. I'm not sure if she wants to kiss me, so I force myself to stop looking at her lips, and look her in the eyes. She nods, just a little bit. That's a yes. She does want me to kiss her. Smiling, I lean forward the couple more inches until my lips touch hers. She barely has time to react before I pull away. Just long enough to know our lips really did touch. Penny wiggles out of her arms and runs out of the room yelling "Ewww! Daddy kissed Piper! Kissing yucky!" I feel my face get warm and groan. Just what I needed; announcements that we kissed. Especially for the first time. Especially when I purposely avoided it earlier when I knew my father was watching.

"On that note, we got reprimanded for being so boisterous as well as running and slamming the door and it's dinner time," I disclose. Her face is red too. With that, I take her hand and lead her to the kitchen.

My parents are sitting at their spots at the table, all dished up and waiting for us. I try to look a little bit sheepish after Penny's announcement when we walk in, but it's hard because when my father sees us, I notice him smirk. My mother glares at him and his face drops to a careful, flat affect. He doesn't want to get in trouble too.

I head directly to the stove. First, I grab the plastic plate that won't break if it gets dropped. Half a scoop of spaghetti noodles with just a tiny bit of sauce. Just enough to make the pile of Parmesan cheese I put on top stick to it. One piece of garlic bread before I turn to Penny. "Two hands. Very careful all the way to the table," I instruct. With a nod, she holds both hands out for me to place the plate in. I watch as she carefully turns around and makes small steps all the way to her side of the table, never taking a hand away until she sets the plate down. Good. My father gets up to help her with putting on an apron to help keep her clothes clean. She's only wearing leggings and a long sleeve shirt, much like Piper's outfit but more colorful, but my mom doesn't like messy eaters and I'd be the one trying to get the spaghetti stain out of her clothes.

When I grab the next plate, I look toward Piper. She's distracted watching Penny, so I dish my own first. Two big scoops of noodles and two big scoops of sauce. Two pieces of garlic bread and Parmesan cheese, though less than I put on Penny's. Now, I'll dish up Piper's food for her. That's gentlemanly or something, right? My father dishes up my mother's food all the time. I do a little more than one good scoop of noodles, but then I have to wait for her to do the sauce. The amount of spaghetti sauce you eat compared to noodles is probably a different ratio for everyone. "Just one scoop of sauce," she says when she realizes I'm looking to her, waiting for instruction.

After I pour the scoop of sauce that's more like chili it's so thick over her noodles, I hand her her plate. "I'll let you grab your garlic bread and put Parmesan on if you want," I tell her, grabbing my own plate. Once she finishes dishing up, I head over to the table, placing my plate at my seat so she knows which one is hers. There's only one remaining next to Penny. I'm just glad they put her chair by Penny versus having her sit next to mother. When she sits down, I help her push her chair in before taking my seat.

Once we're all sitting, I take Piper's hand with my left, and mother's with my right. When Piper looks confused, I nod to Penny who's waiting for Piper to take her hand. When our hands are joined, we say the prayer before meals.

As soon as we're done praying, we reach for our forks and start digging in. When I take some of the sauce off the top of mine and start twirling a few noodles around my plate, I see Piper watching us. Penny just uses her fork to take big scoops, take a bite off, and let all the rest of the noodles collapse back on the plate. Piper is stirring her sauce into the noodles like my father does, while my mother and I keep our sauce piled on top and just eat it without stirring it in. Mother is using a spoon to twirl her noodles, where I'm just using the plate. After Piper twirls her spaghetti on her fork against her plate, she brings the fork to her mouth. When she takes a bite, her eyes close and she groans in delight. She takes a sip of milk before trying a bit of the cheesy garlic bread. Again, her eyes close and she looks like she's in heaven while she's eating.

"How did you make the garlic bread?" she asks after she swallows. Crap, I didn't warn her we don't talk. My father politely explains how he made the garlic bread homemade before Piper replies, "I've never had it homemade before. It's delicious!" My father smiles politely and thanks her, before returning to his food.

When I look over at Piper, she's giving me a quizzical look. I just shrug, after all, I can't very well explain why we don't talk when we don't talk. Instead, I nod toward her food, trying to ask what she thinks. She simply nods before going back to eating with a small frown on her face.

Piper looks so uncomfortable, I have to do something. I have to say something. "So Penny, what did you do today?"

Penny pauses in trying to scoop up more spaghetti to look at me. She then looks at her grandparents. She's so confused. She knows we don't talk. "I played! I did puzzles and blocks and cars and dollies!"

"You did all that today?" I try to act shocked. "Did you have lunch at daycare?"

"Uh huh! I had sammich and peaches and juice."

"Did you take your nap like a good girl?" I ask, just trying to keep her talking.

"Nap time is my favorite, Daddy! Jimmy didn't want to. He cried real loud." Penny looks down at her lap as she says this and when she looks back up, she has her bottom lip stuck out in a pout.

"Did that make it hard to take your nap?"

"It did. I getting sleepy." As if on cue, Penny rubs her eyes. Piper has to stifle a laugh with her hand when Penny's hands move back to her lap and show that sauce got on her face when she rubbed her eyes. It must've gotten on her hand while she was eating.

"Oh my," my mother says, exasperated as she pushes back her chair to stand up. She walks into the kitchen and wets a square of paper towel, wringing it out over the sink and bringing it back to wash Penny's face. I'm not sure why she bothers now, when I'll get her cleaned up before she gets into bed anyways. She's just going to keep eating the messy food.

Once clean, Penny apologizes to her grandmother for getting messy and goes back to eating without talking anymore. My mother also glares at me, I'm sure it's somehow my fault that Penny rubbed her eyes and got her face dirty. Next I'm going to get told that Penny shouldn't use body language ever.

Piper just goes back to eating, probably not wanting to be on the receiving end of one of mother's glares. At one point, I have to smile when I see her put spaghetti noodles on top of the garlic cheese bread before taking a bite. She simply raises it a tiny bit toward me as if in a toast and takes a big bite. I have to try that. When I do, I nod my agreement at the combination of food. Throughout eating, I find her foot under the table a few times. The first couple times, I just bump it. I'm not fully used to having the chairs closer together. After that, though, it becomes a game. I gently put my foot on top of hers when she finally realizes what I'm doing. When she does realize, she smiles a little bit at me. She picks up her foot and places it over mine before I take mine back. Nothing like playing footsie to lessen the tension of dinner when we can't talk.

Soon enough, my plate is empty. I'm always the first one done. I don't get excused until everyone is done, or at least, I don't usually. Waiting, I watch everyone else. Piper is close to done and, when she notices me waiting, she seems to speed up her eating just the tiniest bit. Penny looks like she's going to fall asleep any minute now that she's getting a full stomach. It's like any second she'll just end up with her face down in her food because she'll pass out. Meanwhile, my parents are casually eating, looking like they have no care in the world about how long it takes, as long as they wait for their bodies to signal that they're done.

When Piper finishes her plate of food and cup of milk, I ask, "Mother, Father, can we be excused? I never got to give Piper a tour of the house before she was talked into reading a book. After we're done, I'll come back up to get Penny ready for bed.

"You may be excused, just behave yourselves and no more making such a racket as you did earlier this evening," my mother answers.

"Yes, Ma'am," I answer, nodding before I get up out of my chair. I stand quickly before she can change her mind, then help Piper pull her chair back so she can get up since I had pushed it in. I use my head to motion the direction we're going which is straight out of the kitchen to the hallway. As I turn around, I see my father mouth the word behave. I roll my eyes before heading out of the room.

We take a right down the hallway towards Penny's room. Halfway down the hall, Piper pauses at a family picture. Penny was only about two in the picture, and my brother is next to my father looking like his pride and joy. George and I look a lot alike except he has shorter hair. He was never a sports guy so he's skinnier than I was even a couple years ago. It's not that I'm big, but I have more muscle from hockey than George. My hair wasn't quite as long as it is now, but it was past my ears then. In the picture, I'm next to my mother holding Penny. We're all wearing jeans and different shades of red with the girls wearing pink. I can tell she's looking back and forth between George and I.

"My brother, George," Hudson says, coming back to where I'm

standing.

"Is he around much?"

"Not much, he's coming home this weekend for Christmas. It's usually just once a year or so that we see him. He's in his senior year of undergrad." We were never particularly close, but after Maci got pregnant, he started ignoring me, acting like we weren't related. Sometimes I miss when he actually acknowledged me. Sometimes, he actually acted like he liked me. I reach up to touch the edge of the frame. In this picture, you can't see his disdain for me.

I realize I've gotten distracted, and turn to continue down the hallway. "I'm sorry that was so awkward. I didn't think to warn you that we don't talk at the dinner table. It's one of those things you don't think about until someone else is there experiencing it."

"It's okay," she answers. "You tried to make it better, even if you might've gotten in trouble for it."

I nearly laugh, but realize that might seem condescending or something, so instead, I just smile. "I got glared at. You would've known if I was in trouble. Now, this is my room. Nice and close to the room that I actually sleep in half the time." I take her hand and open the door. Stepping through dramatically, I pull her with me.

When she stops to look around, I try to decide what she's thinking. My room is basically the same size as Penny's, but my wall is blue. It seems smaller, though, because I have a queen size bed rather than a twin. Over my bed, there's my last name with a hockey stick underneath it and Wild banners on each side of my name. I have blackout curtains in front of my windows. On the other side over my desk, there's the personalized Wild jersey that my parents got me for my 13th birthday. Number 17 with my last name on the back. Back when they were proud of me playing hockey. On either side of the jersey is a shelf with trophies and medals. Piper walks over and fingers one of the medals hanging down. "They're all from hockey?"

"Well, there's one trophy from when I was eight or so when I was in a piano competition, but then I chose not to play anymore." I walk over and point at the one closest to the door, red with a black base and music note on top rather than the mix of colors from previous teams and a hockey player on top.

"Wow, that's crazy you have so many..." she walks over to the bed now and sits down. "And this little guy?" she asks, picking up the bunny pink bunny that lives on my bed. It stands out against the forest green comforter.

"That's Hoppy. I'm supposed to keep him here for when Penny crawls in with me if she has bad dreams. He makes her happy, and he's a bunny so he hops. Get it?" I smile, taking the bunny out of her hands and making it hop it's way back to it's spot in the bed. Sitting down next to her, I add, "I'm really glad you agreed to come over. I think there's a little girl in the other room who's glad too."

When her face starts to turn pink, she says, "So, how about the rest of the tour?" Maybe she isn't as happy as I am for her to be here. I stand and hold out my hand to help her up as well.

Hand-in-hand, I pull her to standing. As we leave the room, I point out the bathroom between Penny and my rooms. As we head down the stairs, I point out the office through the kitchen, though I'm sure she saw it while we were eating. At this point, she's seen basically the entire upstairs, so we go to the basement. Directly at the bottom of the stairs is the bathroom we redid a few years ago. Now, it has in-floor heating which my mom always talks about how much she loves when she gets out of the shower. To the left of the bathroom is the laundry room. I show Piper the staircase to go out to the backyard, but she has to remind me that we don't have shoes on so we don't want to go out there. "It's nice in winter when we've been playing outside to come in and strip off the wet winter gear in here and put it right in the dryer. In the summer, we come in this way if we've been playing in the sprinkler or anything that might make us dirty so we won't track it in on the carpet. Since it's all hard floors down here, it's easier to clean up the floor when we walk to the bathroom down here to wash off first."

From there, I move to the family room, directly below the living room. We have the comfortable couch, a papasan chair, and a huge bean bag chair scattered around, all facing the TV. There's a sound system and xbox - though we more often use the xbox to watch movies than to play video games. Next to the TV, we have a full bookshelf of movies.

"So, there's three bedrooms down here as well. The one furthest away from everything is my parents," I explain. "There's also one across the hall which is more of a guest bedroom. And then over here, across from the laundry room, is George's old room." I pull her towards his room and open the door. "You know that staircase outside in the laundry room?" She nods, not sure where I'm going with this. While I continue to talk, I pull her inside the room with me. "That was how the golden child snuck girls in, or snuck himself out to see them. I'm still not sure my parents have figured it out, but I did. My room is right there." I turn to face her and point up at the ceiling, even though we can't see anything in the dark. When she laughs, I'm not sure I can help myself anymore. I take a step forward, only vaguely knowing how close I am by our linked hands.

"Hi," she says. I feel her warm breath on my face. She must be close to me.

"Hi there," I whisper.

"Whatcha doing?" Is this a serious question, or is she stalling?

"What does it seem like I'm doing?"

"It seems like you're probably standing really close to me. You're still holding my right hand. Your other hand is touching my left arm and moving up towards my shoulder."

"Do you always talk when you're nervous?" I ask, pausing my hand on her arm.

"Maybe..." she answers. She sounds like she isn't sure she wants to answer that honestly.

I move my hand up to her face, brushing my thumb across her cheek. When I move my hand toward the back of her head, she automatically starts leaning in towards me. At first the kiss is soft. We're both a little hesitant. I pull away in case she wants to stop. She might not want to go this fast. Instead, she must stand on her tiptoes and she leans back in.

I'm still holding her hand, but I want her closer. I let go of her hand and move it to her lower back, pulling him as close as I can. When I move forward, she takes a couple of steps back until she's pressed up against the wall.

I run my tongue across her lip and she lets me in. She puts a hand on the back of my head, running her fingers through my hair. With her other hand, she's pulling me close with a belt loop. Now, it doesn't matter that I'm wearing jeans and it's harder to tell that I'm hard. She has to feel it with how I'm pressed against her. How does she do that to me so quickly?

Without warning, she uses the belt loop that was pulling me closer to push me away just a little bit. We're both breathing heavily and she leans her forehead on my chest. "Let's go upstairs. You need to get Penny ready for bed," she whispers. I do need to, but I don't want to. I want to spend time with this girl right in front of me.

When she pushes me just a little bit further away, I feel her turn around in my arms. I reach forward for where the door handle is, finding it easily, and turn the knob to open the door. I don't want her to think I'm trying to hold her hostage or do anything against her will, but God, I want to kiss her more. I don't even know what to say to her after that, so I make sure you can't see anything through my pants, and step past her to go upstairs.

I look up when I'm at the table getting Penny to find Piper hesitating, watching us from the top of the stairs. Her lips are swollen from the kissing. Shit, can my parents tell by looking at me too? I should've looked in the mirror before I came up here. Piper turns to look toward the door as Penny hops off her booster seat on her chair.

"You leaving?" Penny asks in a sad, small voice.

"I probably should get going…" she trails off. When she looks up to look at me, I look at my feet. I don't want to keep her here if she doesn't want to be here anymore.

"Read bedtime story? Please?" the small voice asks. "Daddy?" Penny then looks to me, hoping I'll help her out.

"You need to brush your teeth and get your pajamas on before you're ready for bed. Maybe if you can do those things all by yourself, she'll stay to read you ONE story," I say, emphasizing the number. If you let her, she'll pick out five bedtime stories to read.

"Yes, Daddy!" she squeals, running down the hall to the bathroom to start on her tasks.

"You don't have to," I tell her as soon as Penny is out of earshot. "You can leave if you want." I stuff my hands in my pockets. What do I usually do with them? Why do I feel like my hands are just awkward and in the way?

"No, I'll stay and read her a book quick. I think I'd break her heart if I didn't."

I nod my head. She definitely isn't wrong on that. I hope I didn't make a mistake in inviting her here. I hope she'll still want to talk to me after what we just did downstairs. Piper passes me and heads to Penny's room. She kneels near the cloth bins of books on a small bookshelf under the window. The one I see her take out is Goodnight Moon.

Soon, Penny runs into the room with a pink polka dot nightgown on and says, "Teeth brushed! Bedtime!" She clambers into her bed and pulls the comforter over herself. Collapsing onto the pillow, she looks between Piper, still standing near the bookshelf with the book in her hand and me, still by the door. "Daddy, you lay down. Bedtime story." Penny flips her comforter back and moves toward the wall so I have room. Usually she sticks me by the wall, so I'm not totally sure why we're doing this differently tonight.

"I don't know sweetheart..."

"No. Bedtime. Now," Penny says in a bossy voice and points at what is now designated as my spot. Sure, why not? So, I sit on her bed and put my feet up, still fully dressed in my jeans and the nice quarter zip sweater Penny picked out tonight. She covers me up with the blanket, giving me the pillow and using my arm as her personal pillow.

"Piper, sit there read." Penny says, pointing to a spot where my legs are. I wonder if Penny realizes I'm so much taller than her. I mean, my feet are hanging off the end of the bed. Nonetheless, I move my legs over to be closer to the wall so there's space for Piper to sit.

She sits on the edge of the bed in her designated place and opens it to read, barely looking at me. "In the great green room, there was a telephone..."

When I feel something touch my forehead, my eyes flutter open. I must've fallen asleep, again. Piper moves her face away from me and reaches over to touch Penny's hair. She whispers, "See you later, little one."

When she stands, she looks back to me and sees me awake. "Hey," I whisper.

"Hey, I'm heading home."

"Do you want me to walk you out?" I ask, using my right hand that isn't trapped by a child to try to find my way out of the blanket.

"No, it's okay. You sleep more. I didn't mean to wake you."

"I'm not sure I'll be able to purposely sleep with these jeans on. I'll have to go change and then I'll probably sleep in my own bed. This one probably will realize soon enough and find me." I nod towards the sleeping face next to me, smiling when I see how peaceful she looks.

Piper nearly laughs, but stifles it with her hand before whispering, "Well, whatever you decide to do, I need to get home and sleep. We have school tomorrow morning."

Damn, I don't want her to leave. I also don't want to go to school tomorrow, but that's not the important part. I bring my right hand around to gently lift Penny's head before tucking her pillow under it. I have an idea, though. I carefully swing my legs out of bed and ask, "You don't work after school tomorrow, right?"

"No, why?" she asks, sounding suspicious.

"I have a game at 7 tomorrow night, don't suppose you can make it?" My voice is too loud and I feel like I sound too hopeful. When I turn to check on Penny, I see she flopped over to face the wall.

"Shhhhh!" she scolds me. "So, you like me enough to invite me to a game again, huh?"

I stand up, tucking the blanket back around Penny before I answer.

"Maybe I do," I say, pausing to give Piper a quick kiss on the lips, "and maybe I don't." Maybe that's pressing my luck after the basement, but I have to try and hope she'll stick around. I walk past her to my room and pull the third drawer down on my dresser open. When I find a pair of red flannel pajama pants, I toss them on the bed.

"Where is this game?" she asks me. I suppose that's a valid question. I didn't think about that.

"It's actually a home game again. This one is against Piedmont. It'd be really nice if you came." I know I sound like I'm sucking up, but Penny can't come to this game if Piper doesn't. My parents aren't coming tomorrow.

"You are so hot and cold," Piper tells me, leaning against my doorway. I didn't think I was. She pushed me away. I just reacted.

"So are you. Thanks for pointing it out, though. The book got me. So the game?"

"I need to get some homework done first, but I can probably make it."

"I'm going to hold you to that. Now, do you plan to watch me get undressed, or do you want me to walk you out first?" I ask, turning towards her.

"Let's go," she says, turning to head down the hall.

11

When I pull my truck into the school parking lot on Friday morning, I drive a lap around the small parking lot to look for the now-familiar green Subaru. When I spot it, I park right next to it.

Piper must've already gone inside since she isn't in her car, so I grab my backpack from my passenger seat and hop out of my truck. After Piper read Penny to sleep last night, she luckily stayed in bed. I, however, didn't get to go to sleep until a little while later. Either way, we got up on time today.

Inside, I, not surprisingly, find Piper at her locker. She must've just gotten here, because it looks like she's still taking things out of her backpack. "Hey there," I say, trying to sound casual. I rest my hand on the top of her locker door and try to lean on it, but completely fail when the locker door swings open further and I lose my balance. As I right myself, Piper smirks at me. She's so much more reserved when she's at school. I bet something like that yesterday would've made her all out laugh.

"Hey, yourself. You're looking fancy today," she points out. Looking down at what I'm wearing, I find that I do look a little fancy compared to what she mostly has seen me in. I'm wearing a white button-down shirt with black pants, and my black dress shoes. I also have a a seafoam green tie on since that and white are our school colors and am wearing my fleece- lined hockey warm-up jacket over it all. After all, it is January in Minnesota.

"Ahh, yes. That's what you get on game day. Home or away, we have to dress nice," I explain. Home games, people might see us coming into or out of the locker rooms. Away games, they'll definitely see us to and from the bus, plus wherever we get food on our way home.

"Well," she says, pausing before she says more. Is she questioning whether she should finish her sentence? I raise my eyebrows, waiting. When she sees my face, she says, "You do look very nice."

While I'm trying to decide if this awkwardness is better or worse, Leo walks past on his way to his locker and says, "Hey there, lovebirds."

"Does he-" she starts to ask, looking between the boy walking away and me.

"Nope, haven't told him anything. He just knows we've been hanging out a lot this week, though, he may guess if he sees me do this," I say, pausing at the end of my sentence to give her a quick kiss.

"I'm not sure he saw," she answers, face turning pink with embarrassment, despite the small smile that has formed on her lips.

"I'm okay with making sure he has plenty more opportunities to figure it out, if you are."

"I, uh, what about your parents?"

Does she want to come over again? "What about them?"

"Did they figure out that we-"

"That we kissed?" I ask, knowing that's the only way this sentence could go. If she pauses too long in a sentence like that around here, suddenly there's going to be a rumor going around that we did a lot more. "I think they pretty obviously figured out we kissed when they were told."

"I guess," she answers. Was there more to what she's trying to ask?

"I did get The Talk after I walked you out, though."

"Shouldn't it be fairly obvious you know where babies come from at this point?" she asks, turning more red.

"One would think, but maybe they think I forgot. It has been a while, after all." With that comment, her face somehow turns more red. It seems like any and every mention of anything remotely intimate embarrasses her. Honestly, my parents may have only done it in an effort to try to embarrass me and make sure I remembered what happened last time I had a girlfriend. It's not like I can forget when I take care of her, let alone pay the daycare bill. That alone is most of my paycheck.

Piper continues rearranging things in her locker before closing the door and turning to sit in front of it. "So, are you ready to tell me anything about your life yet?" she asks, turning towards me as I slide down the locker door next to hers to sit on the floor.

"Why do you keep asking me at school? I don't want people

overhearing things and giving me shit. I also don't want people to think I'm awesome just because I'm doing all this; I just want them to think I'm awesome anyways." That didn't come out right. I run my hands through my hair and rub my face. When she raises her eyebrows at me, I say, "Okay, sorry. That sounded really full of myself. Do you know what I mean though?"

"I think so. I just don't know when else to ask. I don't want to ask around your parents. Probably shouldn't ask around her. It's not like I see you anywhere else and you don't have time to go out for dinner or anything like that." Seeming exasperated, she leans her head against my upper arm.

Isn't there an obvious way to get information without talking out loud? "You are a millennial, aren't you?"

"What?" she asks, picking her head up to look at me.

"You heard me."

"Aren't we Gen Z?"

"Whatever. You get my point. Just text me. You do know how to text, right?"

"I suppose. How do I know you aren't lying to me then?"

"How do you know I'm not lying to you in person? Also, why would I lie?" Why does she automatically assume I'd lie?

"You're right. I don't know. Although your face would probably show if you were lying to me. And you'd lie because you want to date me."

"I don't think lying is the way you get someone to date you," I answer, standing up as the first bell rings. I hold out both hands to help her up. She places her hands in mine so I can pull her to her feet.

"You're a smart boy," she smiles, standing on her tiptoes to try to kiss me. I debate letting her struggle, but instead decide to stoop down for her to reach my lips. She turns to grab her things out of her locker before turning back to me.

"My lady," I say, holding out my arm for her to take. She does so, giving a little laugh as we start walking.

"Didn't we just decide we're Gen Z? Now you're acting like we're in a different century walking me to class like this." When we get to class, I stop at Piper's desk for her to let go of my arm. She arranges her belongings so that they're just so and looks up to find me still waiting by her.

"Is there something I can do for you?" she asks.

"I don't know," I pause, then smile at her. "I could maybe use payment for escorting you to class."

"Oh yeah?" she asks, smiling back at me. Her smile is bigger this time. It's like I can see the confidence growing in her.

I put one hand on the back of the seat she's sitting in and the other hand on top of her desk. Leaning down, I touch my lips to hers. Her lips move against mine for a second before I hear a whistle behind me. Does he have to be obnoxious? Piper moves her body back against the wall that's behind her, so I turn around to look at Leo.

"You had to, didn't you?"

"I wouldn't say I had to, but you know, I had to." He shrugs, as if he didn't just interrupt us. Sometimes I hate how okay he is with being the center of attention. If he was here kissing Ashley, I wouldn't interrupt them. On the contrary, I'd probably be concerned she'd remember I exist so I might go hide in another room. "So, what did I miss?" Leo asks. Naturally, I reach over across the aisle and smack him across the back of his head. When I look at Piper, she's rolling her eyes at me.

"He was just asking a question. I don't think he really deserved to get hit," she tells me. I smile at her and shrug.

"I think more people are wondering the same thing," Leo adds. Piper and I look around to find about half of the class watching us.

"I think everyone thinks you're saving it for marriage and that's why you won't go on dates with anyone," Piper jokes, obviously trying to give me an excuse in front of everyone.

"Is that not the case?" Leo asks. That's it. I hit him in the back of the head again, this time a bit harder. Leo shakes his head to clear it. "You may look more muscular, but I could probably take you down." Doubtful.

Laughing, I say, "You deserved that last one. Plus, you're not going to take me down before the game tonight. You guys would get killed without me. Plus, I need to get at least two goals again so that I don't let anyone down!" Piper's smile is so bright, I can feel it shining at me. I hadn't even mentioned scoring for her tonight.

"So how did this all come to be? Three days ago, you first met and now today you're making out?

"Leo," I say, trying to take the attention, "if you consider that to be making out, I'd suggest you go find yourself a girl to learn what making out really is. I kissed her, which is also all that happened last night."

"I never said anything more happened considering I didn't know about last night," Leo says, trying to sound innocent. I know better, though.

"You didn't say it, but I got those vibes." Leo simply shrugs before pulling out his phone and starting to aimlessly scroll.

Perfect time to change the subject. "Now Piper," I say seriously. "Turn around. I need to practice my braiding some more."

*****

12

"Why do you talk to the new girl so much?" Ashley asks me during 3rd period. We're lab partners in Chemistry. Sitting at the back of the classroom at the black lab tables, she moves her stool closer to me so our shoulders are brushing. I turn to face her so we aren't touching, but realize that puts her face way too close to mine. Instead, I try to move my stool away from her.

If we keep going like this, by the end of class, I'm going to be falling out of the lab area entirely. Ash is fine, but I don't need her quite that close. "She's nice. Plus, she went to my game." I go back to working out equations. I won't mention how much I like her.

"I go to your games, too. You don't kiss me," she whines, leaning closer to me.

"You go because you're cheering, not because you want to. You should do your work before class ends."

She pouts, which is definitely cuter on Penny. "Can't you help me? You're so smart. I don't get any of this."

"You understood just fine earlier when Ms. Lamb was going over it."

"You know the assignment is harder, Hudsey."

"Actually, I think it's easier." Isn't that the point? You do hard equations in class so you can definitely do the ones on the worksheet.

"Go ahead and finish up the problem you're on and start packing up, class. Just one minute until the bell rings," Ms. Lamb announces. Her brown hair is in a bun and her cardigan is draped over the back of her office chair so she's down to just her dress pants and a nice shirt.

Ashley's stuff is stacked together before the sentence finishes coming out of our teacher's mouth. Guess it's easy to pack up when you're not in the process of working on an equation. I write the last two numbers of the step I'm on and put a star next to the step I'm on so that I don't forget later before closing the black cover of my notebook and putting the cover on my calculator. The calculator cover has a character from one of the more recent superhero movies taped to the back. All of the calculators in this classroom have different characters taped to the covers. Some of the girls grab their favorite characters as soon as they walk in the classroom, even if we don't need calculators that day. I press on the eraser of my mechanical pencil and put the tip of the lead into the desk to retract it.

When the bell rings, we jump off our stools, drop calculators in the basket near the door, and head down the hall. Ashley sticks by me as we walk down the hall and then up the ramp to the cafeteria. As we walk in, I notice that the line is nice and short. That's why we don't go to our lockers, to have less of a line when we get here. It'd take too long to pass the cafeteria, go to our lockers, and get back here to get in line. We drop our class supplies at our table in the center of the cafeteria, my usual spot being the center of the table, before getting in line.

I type my lunch number in, grab a tray and a milk, a napkin, fork, and head to the window. Cheesy garlic bread, marinara sauce, corn, and salad. I wish we got dessert. As good as this lunch is, I want something sweet after I'm done with my meal.

I let them add everything to my tray before heading to my table – with a detour to put some ranch on my pile of lettuce. When I sit down on the bench at the table empty other than school supplies, Ashley sits down next to me. Good thing we're sitting in the middle, if we both sat on the end like this, the table would probably fold in half.

I eat my salad first, then move to corn. Vegetables are most important, right? By the time I'm about to start on my cheese bread, Piper has finally received her lunch and is looking around. I don't think she knows where to sit. She looks at me and still doesn't come over. Doesn't she want to sit with me? I know we haven't sat together yet, but she doesn't seem close to anyone else. I'm not even sure where she's been sitting up until now.

I stand up to go to her. Maybe she doesn't want to sit with all the other people who have accumulated here. She knows Leo and Ashley at least. And, some of the other people sitting here are probably in some of her classes. I'm sure there's somewhere else we can sit if she doesn't want to sit here. I pick up my tray to bring it with me and am startled when it gets pushed back down to the table.

I follow the pink manicured nails on my tray to Ashley on my right. "Where are you going? You haven't finished your lunch."

"I'm going to check on Piper."

"She's just fine. She can stand upright. She can eat on her own. She made it to 17 or 18 or whatever. Leave her alone."

"She doesn't have anyone to sit with. I want to go sit with her. Plus, I shouldn't have to explain myself to you." I pick up my tray again and she pushes it down onto the table again, this time with more force.

"You're a lot more likely to get what you want from me," she says just before she grabs my shirt, pulling me towards her, and kisses me. What the fuck?

I try to take a step back, but instead, I run into the bench behind my legs and collapse. At least it got me away from her grip. Everyone at our table is silent and staring at me. I stand up again and grab my tray. Now I'm really getting out of here. This time, she just tries to grab the tray from my hands. When I pull back on the tray, she pulls harder. You know what? Fine. I let go of the tray. She screeches as the marinara sauce and my cheese bread fly onto her shirt.

The cheese bread obviously doesn't stick, but the marinara sauce does, and then it starts dripping. Right down the center of the white shirt she's wearing. Serves her right. I guess I don't have to bring my tray with me now. Instead, I just grab my stuff from Chemistry and walk over to Piper. I feel all eyes on me with Ashley still yelling, but I don't really care right now. Piper's eyes are wide and her mouth slightly agape. What did that look like to everyone else? Shit, I look back and Leo, still sitting at the table, looks horrified. Hopefully this makes her leave me alone and he'll have a chance, now.

"Let's go somewhere else," I suggest to Piper.

"Umm, yes please," she answers, turning to dump her entire tray. She only saves the carton of chocolate milk before we head out.

Once outside of the cafeteria, we walk out right out the front doors. Everyone in our lunch is allowed to leave, however, no one is allowed to drive. On foot, you can only get so far. The grocery store, the gas station, a restaurant, and a coffee shop.

"Streetcar?" Piper asks about the local restaurant as we turn the corner, heading up to the main road.

"We would've had to call ahead to get our food and get back before Calc. How about we just go to the gas station?"

Piper nods her assent as she tucks the chocolate milk in her sweatshirt pocket. Placing my hands on her shoulders, I move her to the right and take her left hand, walking alongside her. When she looks quizzically at me, I say, "I want to be closer to the road. That way if someone suddenly comes flying and is going to hit us, they'll hit me first. You'll have time to get away."

I barely catch a glimpse of her cute, sheepish smile before she lays her head against my arm. Her head only stays there for a moment, since it's uncomfortable to walk like that, but my shoulder feels cold when she takes her head away again. She can't move too far away, though, since her small hand stays firmly wrapped in mine.

We jog across the main road to the gas station and slip inside the door.

"Go find something to eat. I'll pay," I tell Piper when she pauses inside the door. She opens her mouth to argue with me, but I interrupt. "No, you're getting food. I'm paying. You threw away your entire lunch."

When I wander away, my phone vibrates. When I check it, there's a text from Piper. "Holy, dad voice." My face feels warm as I look up to the hot case, trying to decide what I'm going to get. I pick a burger and go to find a bottle of water. When I meet Piper back by the cash register, she's holding a lunchable.

Everything is put in a bag as I pay and we walk back, making sure she's on my left this time. Always on the inside. Back at the school, we sit on the built-in benches of the cold, metal, picnic table. There, we eat, and she pulls the chocolate milk out of her pocket.

When we're finished eating, we replace everything back in the plastic bag we used to carry it. Before we return to the school, I grab Piper's hand and pull her around the corner, right up against the school with me. At first, she argues, but when I bring her nice and close to me, her eyes move straight to my lips. My hands on her hips, she brings her hands up around my neck to pull me down and bring my lips to her level. She gets just a little taller as she stands on her tip toes and those beautiful, brown eyes close as her lips touch mine.

We don't get to kiss nearly long enough, or privately enough, before the bell rings to head to classes. We drop the garbage in a can and then head in one of the side doors that are closer to our lockers. Inside the first set of doors, a couple of the guys on the team are still hanging out. Piper is almost through the second set of doors, when Brayden says, "Hey Hudson." Piper and I both pause at my name. "Did she have your A1 sauce for lunch?"

"What did you just say?" I ask, moving closer to him. He's almost as tall as me and at least 30 pounds heavier, but I don't really care. That's out of line.

"You heard me. You'd like that."

"And you'd like shutting up, so I don't have to make you."

"Hudson," A voice says. I know it, but I don't register it. A hand pulls at mine. I try to pull my hand back, but it doesn't work. "Let's go. He's just an underclassman idiot. Don't listen to him." I finally look back and see Piper standing there, looking concerned.

"You're right, they aren't worth it," I answer, taking a threatening step toward Brayden before I follow Piper into the school. We don't have long before class and I need a distraction. It reminds me too much of four years ago.

*****

I'm 14 and walking towards the cafeteria for lunch at my old school. The sound of Jake's voice makes me shudder a little. Lately, his voice makes me want to go the other way. When I hear what he's saying, though, I realize I need to go towards it.

"Getting pregnant your freshman year of high school. You're just a little slut, aren't you?" There's only one person he could be talking to. He's been harassing me since he found out, too. Somehow it seems like everyone found out at the same time I did.

When I turn to look, there they are. It's only the two of them. Maci's friends haven't been leaving her side lately, but somehow she got away from them today. Now look what happened.

"Travis!" I yell, trying to distract him. It works. He gets a grin on his face when he sees me coming.

"Coming to save your little girlfriend?" he reaches out a hand like he's going to put his arm around her, but she slaps his arm away.

"She's not my girlfriend, but you need to leave her alone."

"Oh, so this little bitch really is a slut. You're not even dating and she's knocked up with your spawn." Why doesn't he know when to stop?

"Would you just shut up?" I say, pushing his chest. He takes several steps back, trying to stay on his feet.

"Does someone still like her?" He makes a kissy face at me and I'm over him. I'm over his making fun of us.

"Does it matter? You're being an asshole." I take a step forward and push him again. Can I antagonize him enough to get him to start a fight? Do I want to? We're on the same hockey team, but I don't know if I can deal with him anymore.

Jake shakes his head at me after he backs up a few more steps. He gives me a Cheshire cat grin. He knows what I'm trying to do. "I'm not going to fight you, man. Not now. I'm not getting kicked off one of the best hockey teams in the state because you're an idiot." His shoulder bumps mine as he walks past, forcing me to turn and see Maci standing there watching us with wide, doe-like eyes. She turns to follow him toward the cafeteria, but I quickly grab her wrist.

"Wait."

"What do you want, Hudson?"

"I want to talk to you about the other night."

"What about it?"

"You really don't want to - you know - keep it?" I look down at my feet. This is a weird conversation for school.

"Like your mom said. It'd ruin our lives."

"That's not- she meant- ughhh. What if you don't keep it? I do." I didn't think this through. Did I seriously just suggest that?

"What?"

"I'll take it. Just me. Not you."

"Can you carry it for nine months, too? Ruin your perfect body? Feel like shit all the time?" Her eyes are blazing. She hates me. It's that simple.

I bite my lip. "I can't, but I can quit hockey to work and save money. I can quit school to raise it when it's born. You don't have to have anything to do with us."

"I don't plan to have anything to do with you anyways," she spits out. It's like she finally really looks at me. "You want it that bad?"

"I mean, I'd rather this didn't happen at all, but since it did, I don't want to lose the chance. Plus, I think my parents would disown me if you got an abortion."

"That's not your choice."

"It's their choice to disown me either way for getting you pregnant."

"I'll think about it," she finishes, walking past me. "Now, I need food if this parasite needs to grow in the meantime."

13

Sitting at my desk after school, it isn't long before I get a text from Piper, "So what are you doing until the game?"

I look around at the piles of different textbooks and notebooks surrounding me before typing out, "Picked up P from daycare. Going home to do some homework and have dinner." Making the decision to eat before I get too distracted, I head toward the kitchen to make some sandwiches.

I only have the plates out when I get a text again, "Fun... So?"

Me: So?

Piper: Are you up for answering questions? You told me to text you.

I cringe a little. I knew this was coming, but it doesn't mean I was looking forward to this. I type out, "Only if you answer questions too." While I wait for her to decide her first question, I start spreading peanut butter on my bread.

Piper sends back, "I guess. P's mom?" She uses the abbreviation of her name that I did earlier. I appreciate that she's at least kind of trying to be cautious. Nothing like time to be honest, though.

Me: She moved away. Didn't want anything to do with her. We could barely talk her into not aborting.

Piper: Omg... Seriously? Like far away? How old were you guys?

Me: A couple hours away with instructions not to contact her. I turned 15 five days after P was born. P was probably from Maci's 14th birthday celebration getting a little wild.

I slather jelly on two slices of bread before slapping a slice of bread with peanut butter on top of each. I leave one plate in Penny's room for her to eat while she plays before I return to my desk. I find the framed 4x6 picture on my desk of me holding Penny when she was first born. I wasn't in the delivery room, but my family and I were in another room that they brought Penny to right away. Penny had light brown hair when she was born, not too different from now. She looks so tiny in my arms. I was terrified to hold her, but so excited to meet her.

Piper: Ummmm.... I appreciate the honesty, I think?

Crap, should I not have said that much? "TMI?"

Piper: Definitely. When is Penny's birthday?

Me: May 16th.

Piper: So, you're 18 now?

I suppose, I just told her my birthday by telling her Penny's.

Me: You got it. You?

Piper: Only 17. My birthday is next month.

Wait, good to know. This is important information. "Wait, what day? I need to know this."

Piper: Oh dear, Feb. 2.

Me: That's only a couple of weeks away. Anything crazy in your life?

Piper: Not really. I work, my dad works all the time. We barely see each other.

That's only one parent being mentioned and she didn't say if she has any siblings. If she thinks I have trouble answering questions, she's worse. She's even being vague while texting. "Your mom?"

Piper: She died a year ago from cancer. That's why I changed schools.

Oh shit. I wasn't expecting that. "Oh, I'm sorry."

Piper: It's not your fault. Now we both should get some homework done before the game.

Rather than homework, I start eating my sandwich and pull out a Walmart bag of my shopping from before I picked up Penny from daycare. I wish I got a discount working at a grocery store, but no luck. Nonetheless, I pretty much just got the cheap stuff.

*****

I double check the floor around me, and finding no more snacks, money, or pieces of paper, I zip up the backpack in front of me. All ready for the game. Shoving the last bite of my PB&J in my mouth, I stand and loop the little backpack onto my shoulder. Across the hall, I find Penelope playing with her doll house. She's wearing a red long-sleeved shirt with a dinosaur and books on it with some grey leggings. "Grab some shoes," I tell Penny. I mostly picked out her outfit so she'd be warm enough, so I'll let her pick her shoes. It helps prevent argument if she gets to pick at least one piece of the outfit. When she grabs a pair of little combat boots, I smile. Warm and cute. She sits in front of me, holding up her feet so I can slide the boots on and tie them up for her.

Once her shoes are on, I lift her to her feet and say, "Off we go."

"Game time!" Penny exclaims as she skips after me toward the door.

"Are we going to win tonight?" I ask her as I head down the stairs, knowing she always gives me the same answer.

"Of course, you're the bestest!" A smile on my face, I grab her bright pink jacket out of the closet. I already have my hockey bag packed and by the door. Picking that up and looping it onto my shoulder, I open the door and follow Penny to the truck. Bag in the back of the truck, I strap Penny into her car seat and put her backpack near her feet. Going around, I hop into the drivers seat and the heat immediately starts blasting as the truck comes alive. Once my seatbelt is on, I pull out of our driveway and head to the rink. It's a extra chilly night at 10 degrees and that usually makes the rink feel warmer.

It's less than 10 minutes before we pull into the back of the parking lot. I walk Penny in the front door and flash her season pass to let her through. She puts her hand on the counter to get a stamp so we don't have to worry about her getting stuck without an adult. "Backpack," I say, holding it up for her to slide her arms in. Kneeling in front of her, I add, "Alright, Peanut, Piper is coming tonight. You wait here for her, because there's a ticket for her in the backpack, got it?"

"Stay here for Piper," Penny repeats, nodding with a look of seriousness.

"Wish me luck?" I ask.

"Good luck!" she says, throwing her arms around my neck. Before releasing me, she leaves a kiss on my cheek. As I stand, I give a quick look around me to make sure no one is paying attention. Everyone who is here so far is pretty involved in their own conversations.

As I turn to go back to the locker room, I pull my phone out of my pocket. Clicking on Piper's name, I type out, "Find P when you get here. My parents aren't here tonight." I pass through the set of double doors, and take a second to take a deep breath. In through my nose for five seconds, hold for at least four, out for eight. Before everyone is in here, it just smells like the ice. Getting into the right mindset. It'll be fine. Piper will be here to be with Penny, Jake might not even recognize me anymore when my parents have intentionally held me out of this game the last two years. I'm bigger than I was more than three years ago. If he tries to start shit, I can take him. I wasn't staying out of the game against my old school again, I just intentionally didn't write on the calendar who the game was against tonight.

When I get back to the locker room, the first thing I find in my bag is my noise canceling headphones. As soon as they're over my ears, it cancels sound out. Turning them on, I find my pre-game pump up playlist and start my pre-game routine. With a tennis ball I keep in my bag, I grab my stick. In the locker room before people file in too much, I warm up my hands with some stick handling, both on the floor and in the air, bouncing the ball off the blade of my stick from side to side and each side of my blade. Once my hands are warmed up, I write Penny's name on a piece of tape on my stick and tape my stick so Penny's name is safely on the inside. Next, I change into a pair of shorts and a white tshirt. I do a slow jog on the walking track before too many more people show up.

By the time I finish my two slow laps, more of the guys are in the locker room and almost everyone has their headphones on, trying to get in the zone. Scrolling through my phone, I find a specific song. Not everyone would call it a pump up song, but it's about being better than someone who looked down on you. Not only does it seem pertinent when everyone was assholes when Maci got pregnant, but it feels extra pertinent playing my old school tonight. By the time I finish getting dressed and listen to that song a couple more times, coach is telling us to line up for warm ups.

A few minutes into warm ups, I head to the bench to get some water. Really, it's a good time to check on Penny quick. Looking up to the bleachers right near center ice, I find Piper and Penny sitting next to each other. Piper looks up to me, and holds up a twizzler as though she's cheersing me. In the backpack, I planned out snacks for the two of them and when they should open them. Naturally, she was supposed to wait until the first period actually started to grab the first layer, or, I guess it's the second layer since her ticket was first. Ticket, paper telling her to wait until first period and don't dig further because there's something for each period. Penny's doll that we keep exclusively for games - it makes her more fun to play with when she doesn't have her all the time. Twizzlers, a juice with one of those character lids for Penny, and a Dr. Pepper for Piper. I'm not sure what else she likes to drink, but I figured a little caffeine wouldn't hurt her for this game. I do feel bad that with Penny she can't really sit with the other students for an exciting game, but she might need to get away anyways.

I shake my head as I swallow one last sip of water and turn to head back to warm ups. Usually, I like that I'm starter. It means I'm one of the best and I usually get some of the most playing time. Today, however, I almost cringe when I hear my name, because that means Jake might've heard my name and number. He's starting too. He's still playing defense. Great, me versus him. It's only a few minutes into the first period when Leo scores his first goal of the game. Brayden set him up beautifully for his shot from the crease to slide in the lower corner.

A few more shots on goal and even only up 1-0, we're dominating. We've had the puck on their side of the ice at least twice as much as they've had it on ours. During a neutral zone faceoff on our side, Hunter wins and sends it back to Brayden who misses it. I fly back to bring it around the net and back. I have a pretty clear path so I go with it. That is, until I go crashing to the ice. I'm not totally sure what happened, but someone tripped me. When I look up to the player that the ref is leading to the penalty box, it's number 13. That has to be Jake, but at least we have a power play now.

The power play is unsuccessful, but I'm ready when Jake comes out. He definitely knows I'm here now. I don't even care. When Jake has the puck trapped against the board and is fighting for it with Hunter, I check him from behind. "Leave me alone," I say before I let him go. When he turns around, he starts coming at me like he's going to fight me, but I back away, hands up, already heading for the penalty box for my five minutes. When I get out of the penalty box, though, the boys are just collecting themselves behind the net so I'm able to jump right in. With a pass to me, I hit it bar down. After a celebration, I head to the bench. I get my high-five through the plexi-glass from Penny. I may have been sitting the last five minutes, but I'll give someone else a little chance to play.

The zamboni comes out between periods one and two, so we head to the locker rooms. "Hudson!" I hear as I'm zoning out sitting on the bench. Looking up, Coach Fulton is looking at me. "What was that check out there?" I shrug, like I didn't intend to do it. I fully intended to do it. "Well, don't do it again. We can't lose you, even if we're up 2-0 right now. Got it?" I nod in the affirmative. I can't actually guarantee anything. Not with Jake on the other team.

As period two starts, I look up to find Penny and Piper looking in the backpack. "Actually wait for the period to start this time," I wrote on the piece of paper for the second period. Penny is hugging her doll. When Piper shows Penny the two boxes of movie theater candy I got from the store for a dollar, Penny happily takes one. I'm guessing she took the M&Ms. Hopefully Piper likes Cookie Dough Bites. I also put some money for popcorn in the bag for period two. I have to stay in the game into the third period for them to enjoy all their snacks and for Piper to at least get a little bit of warning.

In the first five minutes of the game, the other team scores twice, tying it up. Of course Jake scored one of them. As I see Penny pass me in the corner behind the goal line, though, I manage to set Hunter up for a goal. Goal and assist. I guess we're going Gordie Howe today, but Piper wants a goal too. Penny is holding a bag of popcorn and jumping up and down on ground level by us. 3-2.

Soon after the face off, Jake holds Hunter against the boards. The refs don't even see him. I body check him against the boards and say, "Leave my team alone."

Jake pushes me away and answers back, "It's hockey. They can hold their own, Dad." With another push, I skate away before the refs can throw me in the penalty box again. I have to get that goal for Piper. I have to get that goal for Piper. Before the end of this period. Two minutes later is prime opportunity. We're all in the zone. I pass it to Leo, he passes it back to Brayden. Brayden passes it to Hunter. Just before Hunter gets it, I slide in toward the crease. Hitting my stick on the ground, Hunter sends it to me. One little juggle to make sure I have control before I snipe it in. Got it. One goal for each of them. Now I'm good for next period. Just in time too, because the buzzer sounds for the end of the second period.

Between periods two and three, we sit on the bench while Coach Fulton talks to us. We're up 4-2. Hopefully we can keep this up. I don't want them to end up losing if I get kicked out. I glance up at Penny and Piper to find Piper reading the note. She pulls out the ziplock baggy of chocolate chip cookies. I see her grimace. She saw the ice pack at the bottom, ready for me to pop when I need it. On the note, I warned her to cover Penny's eyes. I don't want Penny to see me punch someone. When

I look to the box next to ours, Jake is practically next to me, right on the other side of the plexiglass. He followed my gaze and is looking up at Penny too. I know he knows, but that doesn't make it better.

It doesn't take long into the third period. I have a breakaway. Maybe I can get a hat trick. Get us a little leeway so my old school doesn't beat us. I veer to the right to be a little further from everyone. Just as I cross the center line, a mass crashes into me. I crash into the boards. Laying on the ice, I can hear the crown jeering. I'm sure it wasn't but that felt like it should've been a penalty. Looking up, I find Jake standing next to me, laughing. "What's wrong? Worried your girl is going to see you get hurt?" There it is. I don't even know if he's referring to my daughter or Piper, but either way, I'm over it. Over him. He needs to leave my girls alone.

Standing, I don't grab my stick. Instead, I throw off my gloves and fly at Jake. Grabbing his collar, I start throwing punches. Right hooks only do so much, so I switch to uppercuts. With that, his helmet comes off. I'm bigger than him now. Enough so that he's barely able to hit me. I'm holding him too far away. After a couple good hits, Jake's knees hit the ground. The refs in my peripheral vision start coming in when he hits the ground, wanting to separate us. I'm surprised it took them this long. I lost focus, though, and Jake is back on his feet. He lands a couple of good punches to my face. When did my helmet come off? Was that just when I hit the boards? My knees hit the ice now. There's a metallic taste in my mouth. My mouth guard is still in my mouth so my teeth should be fine.

Finally, there's a ref between us. One ref grabs Jake, leading him to an exit, another one grabs my arm as I stand, leading me to the door closest to our locker room. I was only expecting to hurt my hand with a couple of good punches, but now my face hurts. I think my nose is bleeding. My ribs hurt. I feel like I'm limping as I leave the ice. It's the ribs. When I lift my hand to my nose to see if it's bleeding, I find a trail of red on my fingers. I need to pinch my nose. See if I can get it to stop on my way back.

Pushing open the door of the locker room, I collapse onto the bench. When I take my hand away, it continues bleeding. First, the athletic trainer comes back. He gives me a nose clamp to put on my nose so I don't have to hold it anymore. That's helpful. I need to leave anyways, so at least this way I can start getting changed. First, I pull my shoulder pads and jersey off. When I peel the white tshirt off from under my pads, the rib pain nearly takes away my breath. "You need to go get that checked at the hospital," the athletic trainer tells me. Damn. Definitely wasn't expecting that. Now it's really a good thing Piper was here.

Next, Coach Fulton comes back. He brings my gloves and helmet, dropping them in the bag I have in front of me. He starts yelling, but I only catch so much of it. Something about him telling me I needed to knock it off earlier. How the hit was legal. Finally, I just break in, "He was taunting me the whole game."

"I don't care," he answers. "This is your team. You take care of your team. Sometimes that means staying in the game."

He doesn't get it. I look pointedly at the trainer, Trey, rather than answering. Coach waves him off, and when the door shuts, I say, "He was the reason I switched schools. He bullied me at my old school. He was starting it again tonight. Just because I have a daughter."

Coach freezes. He looks around like he's trying to figure out who said that. His mouth opens a couple of times before asking, "You what?"

"I have a daughter, Penny. She's almost four years old. She's the reason I changed schools. The reason I was bullied at my old school."

"Where is she?"

"She's in the stands, with Piper."

"Her mom?" I can tell Coach is just trying to make sense of things at this point.

I lean forward to start untying my skates as I say, "No. Her mom isn't in the picture. Piper is, maybe, my girlfriend. I'm not sure yet. She's the only one who knows other than my family."

"Leo--"

"Doesn't know," I finish. I know Leo is his son, but I don't want to lose my best friend.

"You'll tell him?" Suddenly, he seems to have gone from coach to best friend's dad.

"Eventually, I'm sure. Not yet. I guess I need to go to the hospital now," I add the last part flippantly, vaguely waving my hand in the direction Trey went.

"You can't drive."

"Piper can drive me I made sure she came tonight, just in case this happened."

"Just call your mom so she knows what happened," Coach says, opening the door to leave. He pauses, just outside the door. "Piper and Penny?" he asks. "He's inside…. go to the hospital….his ribs…. his head …. calling Beth," he keeps talking, and I only hear bits and pieces as I'm listening to the ringing of my phone.

"Hello?" I hear on the other side of my phone.

"Hi, mother," I say, trying to sound casual.

"What happened?" she asks, already sounding exasperated.

"I'm going to go to the hospital. I may have gotten in a fight and am a little sore." She starts yelling, and I tune out, holding my phone away a couple inches away from my ear.

I hear, "grab her car seat," from Coach before he leaves, but don't even get a chance to thank him in advance for keeping a secret.

"Hey mom," I interrupt. "Mother, Piper is here. I'm sure she's a perfectly safe driver. She'll get the carseat from my truck and put it in her car. We'll drop Penelope off at the house so she can go to bed at a decent time tonight. Then, Piper will drive me to the hospital. I got this." Her voice keeps yelling, but I hang up, looking up as Piper steps in, holding the hand of my little Penny. When Penny steps in and looks at me, she hides behind Piper. My daughter is scared of me.

Piper puts her hand toward her nose and says, "It's probably the blood."

"Oh, yeah," I answer, grabbing my white tshirt. I'll throw the shirt away, but it'll get my face cleaned up a little. I start with dabbing under my nose, but eventually just wipe the entire lower half of my face, hoping that I'm not just smearing the blood. Throwing the shirt toward the trash, I hold out my arms and say, "Come give me a hug, Monkey." When she continues hiding, I opt to get dressed. We need to get out of here before the game ends.

"Coach is pissed I got kicked out," I say. I stand and pause when I sway a little bit, "Do you want to leave while I change?" I ask. Piper eyes me up, and I can't decide if she's checking me out, trying to assess my injuries, or trying to decide how much work it is to help.

"I can help," she answers. Since I'm starting to get stiff, she helps me, with step by step instructions. Breezers, socks, shin guards, more socks. Until I'm left sitting on the bench in just compression shorts. She helps me put my dress pants back on.

Once I have my pants on, Penny starts to look at me like she knows me. The clip can come off my nose. It's hopefully done bleeding. I slide my arms in my dress shirt, bad side first, and start buttoning. At that point, I say to Penny, "Sweetheart, I'm okay." At that, she runs to me, full force. I can't help but let out a little grunt, but engulf her in my hug nonetheless. Her hugs make things better.

"So was the last item for your broken nose or ribs?" Piper asks as she bends down to start stuffing my gear into my bag, including my tie.

"I wasn't intending broken anything. I just had a feeling there'd be a fight of some sort tonight. I was more thinking my hand. I'm glad my parents didn't realize who we were playing or they wouldn't have let me play at all. What I should have packed was something for this headache," I answer, lightly tapping my temple. Piper attempts to pick up the bag, and when it only lifts about two inches off the floor, I can't help but laugh a little. Laughing definitely hurts my ribs, though. "I can deal with that and meet you at my truck if you and P go get your car." Piper looks hesitant to agree, but seems to know that she isn't going to get far with my hockey gear. After nodding, she and Penny head out the door to get the car.

14

Once they walk out the door of the locker room, I breathe a sigh of relief. As sore as I am already, everything is okay. Picking up my hockey bag, I nearly drop it in pain. Instead, I reach for my right side. I have to get it outside somehow and setting it back down isn't going to help me get it there. Instead, I make my way down the hallway to head outside. Before I totally leave, though, I look back at the scoreboard hanging over center ice. Still up 4-2 with two minutes to go. I didn't ruin it for them. With that, I head out, through the throng of people in the lobby where it's much brighter than I've ever noticed, out to the nice darkness, and straight to my truck.

It's once I get to my truck, though, that I realize I may have a problem. If it hurt to pick up my gear bag at all, it's really not going to be fun to try to get it up in the bed of my truck. You know what, though? It'll be better to just get it over with. After I open the back, I pick up an end with each hand, pick it up, and toss it into the back all in one motion. Not only was that horrible for the pain, but a wave of nausea comes over me. I stagger toward the front of the car. There, I take a couple of steps into the snow before lurching onto my knees and throwing up. After my stomach is empty, I opt to lie down for a minute. The cold snow feels good.

Closing my eyes, the day starts to hit me just as a worried voice saying my name hits my ears. I put my hand up to my temple. "Ow." When did that start hurting?

"Oh, thank god you're okay," the voice says again. I think I know that voice, but I can't place it. Opening my eyes, I find Piper kneeling next to me. Someone I can be honest with with the things spinning through my head.

"Okay is relative. I think I have a concussion. At least some cracked ribs. My nose is broken. My coach knows I have a kid. All because I got in a fight with an asshole from my old school," I like to think I sound calm saying all of that, but then it hits a little harder. This is all Jake's fault. I can't help it, I turn to my stomach, slam my fist on the ground and yell, "That fucking jackass!" God, that hurt, both my hand and my head. I probably shouldn't have used the same hand I used to punch him to hit the ground. A bit delayed, I hold my hands to my head. That needs to stop.

"You're getting all wet and you're about to get in my car. Plus, your daughter is waiting on her car seat. You need to get up," Piper says after giving me a minute to ruminate. Looking up at her, I wonder how she's so calm. I'm a train wreck. "You'll never get to the hospital or home if you keep lying here."

"Sorry," I murmur. Standing is rough. I shouldn't have laid down. Even moving my legs makes my ribs hurt, let alone when I move my arms.

At the passenger seat of my car, I open the door to take the carseat out. First, I tug on the seat. No luck. It's buckled in. I click the button to free the seat belt and tug at it from the other side. It still won't come out. When I lean my head on the opening of the door, trying to figure out why this is so hard when I do it daily, Piper says, "Just let me do it. Go get in my car." With a slight nod, I follow directions, practically collapsing into the passenger seat and closing my eyes. Next thing I remember is my left arm being pushed on. Piper is sitting next to me, looking straight ahead. "You need to stay awake. We're not far from your house and then I need to bring you to the doctor. You can't sleep." I nod, but then my arm is being pushed on again. "Stay awake. We're about to pull into your house." When I open my eyes, I see it's true. When I turn around to look in the back seat, Penny is sitting in her car seat. I wonder when Piper did that.

As we come to a stop in the driveway, I tell Piper, "You stay here. I'm going to bring Penny inside. I'll be right back. You stay here." Wait, did I already say that? I frown as I open the door. I need to bring Penny in. I'm going to change clothes. These aren't very comfortable.

When we walk in the door, I stay quiet. Penny and I take off our shoes and hold hands as we climb the stairs. At the top of the stairs, my mother is sitting in the chair with a book. She looks up, seeing us appear, and puts a hand to her mouth. "Your face," is all she says.

"Thanks, mother. Makes me feel great."

It's then that I notice my father on the couch swiveling his head to look at me. "What happened?"

"I got in a fight. Can't you tell?"

"Obviously. Now your nose is going to look like mine. The game shouldn't have been over yet, though. How did you get in a fight?"

"We were playing Piedmont and --"

"You played in a game against Piedmont?" My mother interrupts, shaking her head at me.

"I couldn't skip every game against them. We needed to beat them. I'm good at hockey. I think we won." My voice sounds loud.

"Jake?" my dad asks. When I nod, he adds, "Did you win?" Did I? He got that hit on me, but I think I punched him first. How do you decide who won when the refs separated us? Maybe it was equal?

"I think I won the fight part, but the body check he got on me first probably did more damage than anything." I don't actually remember seeing his face. I could've done more damage than I realize.

My mom shakes her head again. "That was so irresponsible of you to play in that game. You know your temper. You know he knows," she says, looking pointedly at Penny.

"Speaking of Penny, are you guys good to put her to bed so I can go get checked out at the hospital?" I don't want Piper to wait too long, and at this point I just want to get out of here. My mother may seem concerned now, but I feel like it's going to change to being mad before too long. With a nod from my mother, I head to my bedroom. A pair of sweatpants. A fresh pair of boxers. I need a shirt, but I have a feeling a tshirt would hurt to put on. Instead, I grab a zip-up hoodie. I need a shower. I probably reek after the game. Looking in the mirror, I see why Penny was afraid of me. There's still blood on my face. There's a bruise starting to form under my eye. My nose is swollen. When I take off my shirt and look in the mirror, I see that the area of my rib cage that hurts is a little red too. At least it's the opposite side from my tattoo.

My brown hair is slicked back with sweat and partially stuck to the back of my neck. I hop through the shower as quickly as I can manage with the pain, but the heat does seem to help my headache as long as I'm under the water. I have to remind myself that I need to keep getting ready. Piper is waiting for me. At least I look human by the time I get out. Nose is still swollen and the bruises are still there, but there's no dried blood on my face anymore. It's a step in the right direction.

I put my clothes on as fast as I'm able, before heading back to my room. Not knowing what's going to happen, I decide to pack myself some clothes. I don't want to come back here tonight. I can't handle my mother yelling at me more if something is broken. As she pointed out, I know my temper and I don't want to end up yelling at her or something.

Shoving my wallet in my pocket, I grab a handle of my backpack and head out. At the top of the stairs, my mother says, "Keep us updated." Rather than answering, I just wave behind me. My head is starting to hurt again.

Piper's car is still in the same place it was when I came inside when I walk back out. I put the backpack in her backseat before climbing into the passenger seat. When I sit down, she just looks at me rather than starting to drive.

When she finally speaks, she says, "So, you know when we go to the hospital, you might meet my dad, right?"

"Then don't." I don't really care where we go at this point.

"Don't?"

"Don't go to the hospital. Let's go to your house. I just know I'm not going back inside and getting yelled at more with this headache. My mom just kept saying that I was being irresponsible." Grappling for the handle on the side of the seat as she starts driving, I finally find it and put the seat back. There, I close my eyes. After a minute, I notice that I don't feel the telltale bumps of driving down the road. It's a good neighborhood. The roads aren't particularly bad, but the ice pack combined with the regular freezing and thawing every year does do a number to roads. Finally, I open my eyes and look at Piper. She's looking at me, not driving. "Yes?"

"Put the ice pack that you packed yourself on your face because your nose is swelling. We're going to the hospital to make sure you're okay. Then we'll discuss what's happening after depending on what we find out." Rather than answering, I just stare at her. I've never seen her be so assertive other than earlier when she told me to get off the ground. I'm not sure if I'm bringing out the worst in her, or if it means she just isn't scared to be herself around me anymore. Reaching to the backseat, I find the backpack from earlier on the floor still. I forgot to bring it in. Where did I leave my hockey bag? As I fish around in the bag, Piper adds, "We also saved you a cookie for after the game, but you may want to wait just to make sure you're good and don't need surgery of any kind. If you eat now, you won't be able to have surgery for hours."

I can't help but roll my eyes, but luckily she can't see it in the darkness of the car. Instead, I pull the backpack up front with me. That leaning to the backseat hurt my side. First, I find the ziplock bag with the cookie and set it on my lap. When I reach back in, I find the ice pack - the only thing left in there. Dropping the bag on the floor by my feet, I say, "I definitely don't need surgery of any kind. They're just going to tell me everything that's wrong with me after a few scans and we'll be leaving." With that, I pop the ice pack and balance it on my nose before pulling out the cookie to take a bite. I can't believe I gave the girls those cookies. These are good.

When she shakes her head, I almost laugh before saying, "Good, now you know how it feels to have someone blatantly disregard your instructions. At least I wasn't teaching a small child to do the same thing."

"No, but you knew your child that you were supposed to drive home after the game was in the stands when you got in a fight."

I get the point. Both her and my mother made that point. "Like I said, I wasn't expecting it to be that bad. Maybe just a couple punches. Definitely nothing that would throw me out of the game. Or inhibit my driving. Plus, she's usually sleeping by then and I knew you were there anyways." I shrug, trying to seem nonchalant. She is usually sleeping and I made sure Piper would be there. I wasn't going to take Penny to this game if Piper wasn't coming.

Piper gives a loud sigh before shifting the car back into drive and heading down the road. In less than five minutes, we're at the hospital, but I pretend to sleep on the way. I know I have a daughter. I know I'm supposed to be the good influence. I also don't want to teach her to just lay down and take whatever bullying people throw at her when she grows up, though. Sitting up from the seat laying down hurts. Like a lot more than anything else I've done so far tonight. When I stand up out of the car, I have to hold my ribs. As I start walking, I feel like I'm moving stiffly. Between the ice pack on my face and the way I'm walking, the person at the registration desk definitely isn't going to question if I need to be seen.

Inside, I walk up to the desk straight in front of the door. "What can I do for you?" The woman with short brown hair asks.

I try not to scoff. Is that really a question? "I need to be seen," I answer simply.

"I'll need your license and insurance card, then I'll have you fill out this clipboard."

"Can you find them?" I ask Piper as I hand her my brown, leather wallet.

With a nod, she takes it and opens it up. Almost immediately, she says, "Awwww, how cute." My license is right in front and it's a picture from the day after I turned 16. Maybe I should've found my own cards so she didn't see that, but this way I can keep holding the ice pack on my face. After some more sifting, she pulls out a couple more cards. The woman behind the desk sifts through the cards, pulling out one and getting up to a copy machine. When she returns, I see that she photocopied the license and medical insurance. She hands the stack of cards back to us, along with a clipboard and a pen. I set the ice pack aside to fill out the clipboard while Piper shoves the cards back into slots.

"Piper?" I hear a voice say behind me. Rather than looking, I focus on my paperwork. I assume it's Piper's dad, and maybe if I take long enough filling out the paperwork, I won't be noticed. Name, birthday, social security, address, phone number. Emergency contact. I guess I pretty much have to put my parents, but I'll choose my father. Signature. Crap, that was too quick. I hand my clipboard back to the woman, thanking her as I pick up my ice pack again and, as I turn toward Piper, I notice her pointing toward me. When she looks at me, I see a little cringe.

"That's the adoring look that I love to see on your face," I joke. When I look at her dad, though, I pause. Maybe I shouldn't have said that. He's a tall dude and not particularly skinny. A bit intimidating if I'm being honest. Close cropped hair. His face is mostly shaved other than his mustache and beard in a circle around his mouth and he's wearing a security uniform. "Oh, hi, I'm Hudson," I say as I move my left hand to hold my ice pack as I hold my right hand out to shake hands.

Her dad holds his hand out as well and looks to Piper to ask, "How do you two know each other?"

"We just have a couple of classes together," she answers quickly before adding, "I was at the hockey game tonight when he got hurt. His parents weren't there, so I offered to drive him."

He gives me a look as though I'm going to corrupt his daughter before asking her, "You gonna be home for dinner tomorrow?" She gives a quick answer about working before he walks away and she collapses in the nearest chair. I follow her to the next chair and sit as gently as I can to minimize my pain. "Probably not the best first impression?" I ask, trying to relieve some of the tension.

"I think I won for the better first impression, even if I was a little too casual. At least I didn't have broken bones, a concussion, and a black eye forming. Even if you are still able to be your normal, charming self." Even though she's right, I act offended. With that, though, we fall silent while waiting for my name to get called. After a lot of questions, a series of scans, and a long time waiting for results of the scans, we learn that I only bruised my ribs, my nose might be broken but they wouldn't do anything about it today, and I have a mild concussion.

As we get into the car to leave, I say. "You know, I was serious earlier."

She pauses buckling her seatbelt to look at me. "About what?"

"Not wanting to go home. My parents have Penny tonight. Plus," I pause, touching her arm, "your dad is working and it'd be a good opportunity for us to get to know each other." Now that the hospital part is over, I can think about other things.

"I don't know. I work tomorrow at eleven and it's already pretty late." She pointedly looks at the radio of the car. When I follow her look, I see the time is 9:45. How did that happen?

"I was supposed to work tomorrow. I probably shouldn't now. Too much thinking and physical work. Even if my ribs aren't broken, the doctor did say I should take it easy and not play hockey for a couple weeks for my ribs and brain to heal. I think that would include needing to rest and not stocking or anything."

"I think you're going to have a problem," she says out of nowhere.

"What's that?"

"That also means you can't lift up your daughter."

I drop my head back against the seat, making it feel like my entire brain vibrated inside my skull. "Oh, God. She's going to hate that."

"You probably shouldn't hit your head against the seat like that," she points out, shifting the car into drive.

"Probably not wrong," I mutter under my breath, closing my eyes and reaching to lean the seat halfway back again. When the seat moves back too quickly, I reach to splint my side like the nurse showed me to. "This is gonna suck."

It's a good 20 minutes before we get to her house. I didn't realize she lives way out here. At least 10 minutes the opposite way from me when we leave school. That's not convenient for her going to work. When we pull in the driveway, there's trees surrounding the house on either side with a wooden fence just inside both tree lines going to the garage that's practically in the backyard. The house is a dark green with a huge weeping willow tree in the middle of the front yard. I can only see so much by the motion lights that came on when we pulled in since it's dark outside.

Without a word, Piper gets out of the car, so I follow her lead, grabbing my backpack from the back seat where I put it when I came out of my house. We go up the deck and in the side door. Inside the side door, the kitchen is to my right, the living room to my left, and a wall directly in front of me. We both remove our shoes, and Piper pushes mine into the corner with her tennis shoes stacked on top of them. She's trying to hide me.

When she steps to the right into the kitchen, I follow her. She pauses at the fridge and pulls an ice pack out, turning to a drawer behind her where she pulls out a kitchen towel to wrap the ice pack. "You can decide if you want it for your eye, nose, or ribs," she says, shrugging. I test to see if the ice pack is flexible. When I learn it is, I put it on my face with it bent around my nose and enough tail to ice my left eye too. She heads the other way out of the kitchen and says, "Now this way. Obviously, that was the kitchen. We have the dining table. Living room is to the left. Down this hall we have the bathroom, office, dad's room, and, finally, my room." She points at each room as we pass them, without giving me a chance to look at them.

When she goes into the room she pointed out at hers, I pause in the doorway. She walks straight to a dresser where she starts sifting through the drawers without saying anything. When she turns around holding a couples pieces of clothes, she looks at me and asks, "You gonna come in?"

"Can I?" How am I supposed to know I can come in her room?

"Uh, yeah? You're coming over to sleep, right? This is where the bed is. Unless you wanted the couch..." She looks like she's questioning every thought she's ever had.

To save her from overthinking, I quickly answer, "No, we can share the bed." I was hoping for that anyways, but I wasn't going to ask.

"Okay, I'm going to the bathroom to change into my pajamas. I also need to wash my face and brush my teeth. You can change in here." With that, she brushes past where I'm still standing in the doorway. After she leaves the room, I continue inside.

Her walls are a muted but light blue. In front of a window, straight out from the door is her bed, long end pushed up against the wall. Her closet is to my left and to my right is her dresser and a bookshelf just about filled with books. The brown bookshelf has 3 shelves and is about 4 feet tall. On top, theres a bunch of picture frames. Stooping to glance through the books, I find that there's a lot that I've heard of, though, most of the ones I know are also movies. The Hunger Games, The Fault In Our Stars, Along For the Ride, If I Stay, The Princess Diaries, and The Kissing Booth. Some of them have other books by the same authors - sequels maybe. I've seen the movies of a lot of these, but I never did see The Fault In Our Stars when it was popular. I don't even know what it's about, so I pull it out and stand up straight while I read the back. Maybe I should read it if she likes it.

When I look up, I find myself looking at the pictures. There's one where she's probably elementary school age, grinning at the camera with a blonde girl at an angle that makes me think one of the girls took the picture themselves. In another, the same two girls are sticking their head out of a window up high in what looks like a clubhouse or something. Finally, I notice one where Piper is probably the same age as Penny. Her mom then looked a lot like she does now, with her hair just a few shades lighter and cheeks a little skinnier. Piper has more freckles than her mom, too. I pick up the frame to look at it closer and smile when I notice the bright pink frosting on the tip of Piper's nose. They must've been baking. After I notice that, I see that there's white that must be flour on her little green shirt.

I get that prickly feeling on the back of my neck like I'm being watched, so I say, "You were a cute kid, you know that?"

"As opposed to?" She walks up beside me to look at the frame in my hand.

"You know what I mean. You look pretty similar to how you do now but just in a little kid version. It's adorable. I'd say you almost compete with P for cutest kid." With that, I set the frame back in it's place in the dust print on top of the bookshelf.

"I bet you were cuter than either of us. You practically have to have been a cute kid to have a cute kid. So, what do you have in your hand?" she asks, turning quickly to attempt to snatch the book.

"Nothing, I don't know what you're talking about." I hold the book in the air where she can't reach it. I can feel it in my ribs and I'm not even holding it with the side that I hurt.

"The Fault in Our Stars? You haven't read it yet? I have like all of John Green's books."

"I saw a lot on your bookshelf. This looks like a well-read one, too." When I bring it back down to a normal level, I hold it flat in my hand. The book pages aren't all pushed together like a new book, they're separated like they've been opened a couple dozen times.

"You can read it if you want to. Now are you planning on changing?"

I forgot I was supposed to change when she was gone. I got too distracted by her bookshelf. "I was, and I brought pajama pants. I just wasn't sure..."

"Wasn't sure about what?"

"I don't usually sleep with a shirt on. I don't really want to sleep in the sweatshirt because that seems hot and uncomfortable. I'm just not sure about putting my arms into a t-shirt with my ribs either." I shrug, trying to leave it open ended, but look between Piper and my backpack I dropped in the middle of the floor at some point.

"It's not like I haven't seen you without a shirt on since I helped you change," she says it calmly, but a blush creeps up onto her cheeks.

Agreeing, I nod and unzip my sweatshirt. Piper sets her phone on a wireless charger on a night stand near the head of her bed before she crawls into bed. She goes all the way to the side near the window before laying down to face me. Focus Hudson. The nurse said it's better to do my good side first when getting undressed. I take my left arm out of my sweatshirt with minimal incident, then let go of the sweatshirt so it's hanging on by my right arm. From there, I can just pull it off my arm. Dropping the sweatshirt on the floor next to my backpack, I kneel to see what I packed. I didn't pay much attention and it's a pair of pants that barely fits me. "I could just sleep in these," I say, looking down at my sweatpants.

"You could. It's up to you if they're comfy enough to sleep in," she says, snuggling her head down into her blue, plaid pillow. I didn't notice until she had pulled the blankets back, but the sheets and pillow cases are matching flannel. There's three blankets stacked atop each other on the bed. I only have my one comforter and sometimes don't even use that.

Deciding to just stick with the sweatpants, I stand. When I drop my phone on top of hers and sit on the bed, Piper says, "Wait."

"What?" I freeze. She did tell me I can sleep in the bed, right? I didn't mishear?

"The light. Last one in bed turns off the light." She points at the light switch next to the bedroom door while trying to look extra comfy in the bed.

"You're going to make the one who doesn't know your room turn off your light and then walk back to your bed? What if I trip and really do break my ribs this time?"

"You won't break your ribs from falling from a standing position. You aren't a giant. Plus, it's a clear path." She uses her hand to make a shooing motion toward me. Standing, I assess the floor to make sure I'm not going to trip. There's very little on the blue carpeted floor, so I move to the door. "You'll be fine as long as you don't walk straight into the wall."

"Well, then I'd definitely break my nose!" I answer, double checking the direction of the bed before dramatically touching my nose and flipping the light off.

"We don't actually know that your nose isn't broken right now. You'll find out in a week when you go back to your regular doctor to have it looked at." I forgot about that part of the visit.

My hand out in front of me to find the bed, I climb in and lay down next to Piper, on my left side facing her, before I answer, "That is, if I decide to have it looked at. I don't know that it's worth it to get it fixed and have to wear a splint on it for a week or two afterwards. Plus, this way I'd match my dad with a crooked nose."

"You don't want your nose straight if that's an option?" she asks, sounding genuinely confused.

"What? You don't think I'd be as good looking with a crooked nose?"

"I didn't say that," she says, probably trying to not offend me.

"It's not so much about the shape of my nose. If I have a splint on, my coach probably won't want me playing. I'll be okayed after a minor concussion before then. My ribs will hopefully be good enough before then to be able to play since we wear so many pads. It's not like basketball or something where we hit each other directly. I don't want to be waiting on my nose when I'm under my helmet anyways."

"You thought about that a lot already." I've always been good at explaining things enough that it makes sense to other people, even if all my thoughts are a cluttered mess in my head. In the silence, I feel her hand touch my chest. She moves her hand hesitantly, before pulling it back. I like the feeling of her skin touching mine. Finally, she breaks the silence. "So, do you want to talk about what happened tonight?"

"What about it?" I ask, capturing her hand in mine.

"Well, you knew you were going to get in a fight of some sort – even if you didn't know to what extent. I want to know why and who it was. Did you know it would be that person or just anyone from that team?"

She throws questions at me so fast, I can barely keep track of what she asked, so I just start to explain, "I mean, it really could've been anyone on that team, though I suspected it'd be Jake. Jake was one of the guys who was the worst to me after Penny was born. You see, that was my old school we were playing tonight. None of the guys on my team now knew that it was my old school, though. At least, I don't think so."

"So, if that guy bullied you at your old school, I'd expect you to go after him. But he seemed to be going after you more."

"I mean, I think he was trying to antagonize me with that first hit. Then I checked him from behind and they all recognized me if they hadn't already recognized my name in the line up. I realized my mistake after that because then most of their attacks were subtle and they started directing them at the whole team. Obviously, you saw the culmination of it all."

She lets go of my hand and rubs her hand up and down on my arm in a comforting gesture. "So, Leo didn't know anything about it?" Piper asks after a minute to digest what I said. "He just jumped in to help you like that?"

"He tried to help me? I didn't even see." He texted me earlier to check on me, but I didn't answer.

"Another guy from the other team got involved too and the refs pulled them apart pretty much right away. Then, as I was leaving, I saw those two were in the penalty box. That Jake dude was ejected too."

"I should text him and thank him," I decide, rolling over to find my phone. Pain erupts through my side when I roll onto it, and I have to stop and let out a groan.

"Did you forget about your ribs?" Piper asks with a hint of a laugh in her voice. I simply groan out a yes as my full answer. "The doctor did mention it might be better to sleep on the side with your injured ribs. Something about it helping you breathe better."

Giving up on trying to get my phone, I roll back over to face Piper. "But that hurts. Plus, then it's harder to try to sneak a kiss from you." I gently shimmy my body closer until I can feel her breath on my face. Bringing my hand up to her face, I brush my thumb against her cheek bone and use my hand as reference as I lean in to kiss her. She doesn't hesitate to kiss me back. As I deepen the kiss, she brings her hand up to my neck. She kisses me for another minute before pulling away.

"We probably shouldn't," she whispers.

"We shouldn't kiss?" I ask, pressing my forehead against hers.

"Not when it's raising your heart rate like that. The doctor said don't do anything that will raise your heart rate for a little while. It'll help your brain rest or something."

Raise my heart rate? "Wait, did you just check my pulse?" I asks. I find her hand on my neck and realize that's totally where her hand is.

"Maybe..." she answers, hesitating.

"Well, how about one more nice kiss and then I'll lay on my back to sleep," I say, just wanting another kiss at this point, even if that's it. My head feels better after turning off the light.

"Deal," Piper says, leaning forward to give me one more short kiss. "Goodnight."

*****

When I wake up, it takes me a minute to realize where I am. I'm laying on my back in a bed in a strange room. When I look to my left, I can't help but smile. Piper. I'm at her house. In her bed. Why am I here, though?

Turning onto my left side, I realize my right hurts. That's right. The fight.

I just manage to get comfortable on my left side before her eyes open. "Good morning, Beautiful," I whisper, realizing my voice definitely sounds like I just woke up.

"Good morning," she answers, giving a tiny smile before a frown appears between her eyebrows.

Reaching my thumb to try to smooth the skin, I ask, "Why are you frowning?"

"I don't usually smile for at least a couple hours after I wake up. I'm not a morning person."

"That doesn't seem like a reason to frown though?" I ask, confused.

"It's more that it confused me – not that I'm upset about it." She shrugs before giving me another small smile. When we hear a cough, her smile disappears and she says, "We should get up, though. I probably work soonish." With that, I sit up, splinting my ribs, for her to get out of bed around me.

Rather than collecting her clothes and going to the bathroom to get ready, she creeps out of the room, looking like she's taking care of where to step. I obviously shouldn't be here. I should find my clothes. While she's gone, I hear a hacking cough that obviously isn't hers, but no words are spoken. I shimmy out of my sweats and pull jeans on. Why did I pack jeans? I'm not even being careful. I'm just trying to get ready so we can leave if I'm not supposed to be here. Piper returns with my shoes in hand as I'm forcing my tshirt over my head - holding my breath. After that, I have to pause and take a few breaths to let the pain go back down, then I can pull the shirt the rest of the way down. Next, I put my zip up sweatshirt over my right hand and up my arm before reaching with my left to get it on all the way.

Piper pushes the door closed before whispering from just inside the doorway, "You don't need to rush. I need to get ready too."

"I saw you sneaking around out there. I don't want to be the reason you have to sneak in your own house." With the sound of footsteps in the hall, she holds up a finger, signaling for me to stop talking.

The sound of a door clicking shut is heard before she whispers back, "I need to get ready for work, though, then I'll drive you. Chill." Moving her hand down through the air, I get the idea. Calm down. She pulls clothes from her dresser, opening each drawer from top to bottom. "Stay here. I'm going to brush my teeth." I put my shoes on while she's in the bathroom getting ready. As soon as she comes back, we each collect our things - phone, backpacks, and keys in her case, and we're out the door, walking silently but not running into anyone. It smells like cigarette smoke out here now and the tv is still on SpongeBob.

15

"Where were you?" I hear screeched as soon as I walk in my front door. I cringe and stop, taking off my shoes in the doorway. I don't see my mother, but I know her. She's sitting at the formal table. The only times we use it is when father has his fancy coworkers over, or when I'm in trouble. The last time it was used for me, was when they found out about Penny. At least that time, I wasn't the only one under the age of 40 at that table, Maci was there too.

"I wasn't here?" I know this will only make her more mad, but I can't help it. Part of me has to say it. I practically hear her growl as I walk up the stairs. If only my room were in the basement so I could avoid her.

I turn left at the top of the stairs to go to my room and hear, "No. Turn around and sit down." I could be a child and sit on the floor after I turn around, but that probably wouldn't help my situation. Also, getting up from the floor might be painful. Maybe sitting down, too.

I had avoided even looking, but I was right that she was at the formal dining table. So is my father. Therefore, Penny is here. Couldn't one of them have taken her out at least? They're at either end of the table, so I have to sit between them. This isn't good. Not at all.

I finally trudge over, pulling out a chair and sitting down. "Good morning, mother and father. I hope you slept well."

"Cut it," my mother answers curtly. I lean away, taken aback. Is she somehow more mad than she was about Maci getting pregnant? "Where were you last night?"

"I stayed at Piper's house after we left the emergency room. I knew you were angry, so I was trying to delay the inevitable."

"And does that seem like it was a good idea?"

"Honestly, it was nice to get to know her a little more. Especially since I figure I'm in more trouble now than I was in before."

"Getting to know her will be awfully hard without a phone," my mother agrees.

Putting my head in my hands, I ask, "Would I have lost my phone if I hadn't stayed at her house?"

"After you deliberately left out who you guys were playing? Were you intending to get in a fight last night?"

"My own parents don't even check the schedule to see who we're playing! And, I wouldn't say intending to get in a fight." My father nearly laughs and she gives us both a sharp look. "I knew it was a possibility and was going to allow it to happen. After all, I never felt like I got to tell that asshole what I thought about him. If anything, I thought it might be a couple punches and they'd pull us off each other. I didn't think it'd get this far," I finish, gesturing at my eye. I haven't actually looked at it today, but I'm assuming it looks bad.

"It's not just that though, is it?" She sounds more snarky than concerned, still trying to find out the full extent.

"My ribs too. They say they're just bruised, not broken. I just know they hurt. I can't pick up Penelope and I won't be able to stock. If I talk to someone, I might be able to cashier until I'm better - it was too late to call last night."

"Did you call this morning to tell them?"

"I just told them I couldn't come in today. I wasn't sure past that. I supposedly might have a concussion, too."

"If you do, it's minor," my father says. He would know. "Besides, if I were you, I'd be more concerned that you aren't prettier than me anymore and you can't take care of your daughter."

I roll my eyes at him before saying, "I can take care of her. I just can't pick her up. She's old enough to walk. By the way, where is she?"

"After breakfast we went for a walk to the playground and wore her out. She's napping."

I nod, glad they kept her occupied this morning. "Thank you."

After a little more back and forth, it's determined I won't have my phone and am grounded for two weeks. I'm out of hockey until I'm healed. Other than that, I'm just going to school, going to work, and taking care of Penny. Oh, and Christmas with my grandmother and brother today, but that can also count as punishment.

*****

I hop out of Coach Peterson's car in my driveway. Mother didn't show up to pick me up from practice. I checked the calendar this morning before school. She was supposed to be there to get me. I'm only 14, I can't drive myself yet. Maybe she forgot since it's my first year on varsity and still the beginning of the season.

When I get inside, I shut the door and slip off my shoes. Instinctively, I want to call out that I'm home. Everyone always does in tv shows. I've been scolded too many times for it, though. Scolded that they know I'm home just from the door closing and that I don't need to yell. I don't understand why we can't be a normal family. Why my parents can't be normal. Just because they both grew up in rich circles and were raised like they always need to be fancy, they think we need to be raised like that.

I bring my hockey bag down to the laundry room before I turn around. George's door is open. Leaning in the doorway, I ask, "Do you know where mom is? She was supposed to pick me up."

George looks up from his desk with wide eyes. He simply points upstairs. I frown at him.

"You better go up there." Why do I feel like I'm in trouble? I simply nod and turn the corner to head upstairs.

As I round the corner at the top of the stairs, I slow down. My parents are at the formal table along with Maci and her parents. I've been trying to talk to Maci at school for the last month, but she's been avoiding me, then she disappeared for the last few weeks. She's wearing sweatpants and a sweatshirt - both black today. Her light brown hair is up in a bun. Without any makeup on, her face looks more mousy than ever.

"What's going on?" I pause before I reach the table.

Everyone looks at me as my mom says, "Sit down. We need to talk."

I pull out the empty chair next to Maci and collapse into the chair.

"Can you please sit down nicely? You know better than to treat the furniture like that." My mom scolds me.

"I'm sorry. What's going on?"

"Well, Maci's parents gave us a call earlier and we thought we all needed to have a chat." My dad pauses and looks meaningfully at me. What does this have to do with me?

"Maci…" Her mom says, in an urging tone.

"I'm pregnant," she mutters.

I stare at her. I can barely comprehend what she just said. "We- we only did it once."

She nods. She knows.

My mom interrupts my shock by asking, "When was it?" My face warms. I don't want to talk about this with her. With any of them.

Maci answers the question. "Just before school started." I can tell everyone is mentally doing the math. I am, too. Two and a half months.

"Why didn't you tell me sooner?" I ask. She avoided me when school started, but she wouldn't have known yet.

"I didn't find out until a month ago. I… tried to take care of it myself."

"You, what?"

Her mom interrupts this time. "She overdosed trying to kill herself and the baby."

What? That's why she wasn't at school. Looking around the table, I realize everyone else must've known already. She didn't want a kid so bad, she almost killed herself.

"You two have ruined your lives with that choice you made." Maybe a bit harsh considering what was just revealed.

"I still have a choice I can make in the next couple of weeks," Maci answers. As if she didn't already try to do it once. My mom gives her a stern look.

"You won't make that choice. I won't have anyone in my family making that choice."

"Good thing I'm not in your family then," Maci answers as she stands up, heading straight for the door. Her parents stand to follow her out.

My head collapses into my hands. What did we do?

"You can finish this hockey season, but you're done after that. After this season, you're getting a job. You need to start saving up money." My mom gives no option. These are orders. She decided this before I got home. "This was irresponsible. Especially at your age. Now you won't be able to go to college or have any kind of real career. You'll be lucky to finish high school. She'll be three by the time you finish high school. I don't think grounding you will do much at this point, but having to raise a child at your age will be enough."

*****

This last Christmas celebration of the year is supposed to be special. Everyone is home at my parents' house and it's the last chance to enjoy our tree until after Thanksgiving next year. I dread this one, even though it's practically the only one. They come home, we open gifts, we have a nice dinner, church tomorrow morning, then they (hopefully) leave. The problem is, I'm the only one who really acknowledges Penny. They aren't outright mean to her, but they aren't friendly either. You'd think my grandmother would want to be with her, but no, she ignores her existence. That is, unless it's convenient for her to recognize her existence long enough to say something mean to me. She'll find any excuse to try to make me mad, then she acts like she has no idea why I'm mad. A couple years ago, I ended up packing up Penny and driving around, looking for houses that still had their Christmas decorations up.

My brother is friendly enough, but Penny's existence made his last year of high school more difficult than it needed to be. It was his senior year that Maci got pregnant. No one had anything against him, necessarily, but they said plenty about me being a screw up that he was pretty much sick of me by the time he left for college. He hasn't come home to see one of my hockey games since, even though he was one of my biggest hockey fans before. Now that's Penny's job.

After I'm done talking to my parents, I gather all the dirty laundry between our upstairs rooms, creeping into Penny's room so as not to wake her up. If I'm being honest, I tend to ignore laundry with everything I have, at least, until I'm practically out of clean clothes. Usually, it's the socks that run out first. I never understand. I'm constantly buying more socks. There's enough laundry to fill a laundry basket. Maybe that wouldn't be impressive to most households, but when it's only me and a small person with small clothes, it takes more clothes than you think to fill a laundry basket.

Pushing the laundry basket toward the top of the stairs with my foot, I don't want to have to pick it up. I want to text Piper, but my phone was taken away. Apparently I wasn't being quiet enough, though, because I hear small feet running toward me and the small voice asks, "Daddy, rollercoaster?" She's standing next to the laundry basket, so I look around. I don't see either of my parents. Where could they be, though? The guest room should already be set up, so I don't think they're downstairs. Just as Penny is about to climb into the laundry basket, I see a car pull into the driveway through the glass in our door.

"Sorry, Monkey. Too dangerous," I tell Penny. "Daddy can't pick you up, though." She pouts, climbing out, as I step in front of the laundry basket and drag it down the stairs. I occasionally let her sit in the basket and ride it down the stairs, but not only will we get in trouble with my parents for it being dangerous, but I think my grandmother would think I'm trying to kill my daughter. I'd rather the luck be on my side and my daughter in the laundry basket plows her over on her way inside. "Can you go make sure your bedroom is picked up?" I ask, trying to give her a way to get out of Judy's way. Internally, I call her Judy. It's my way of getting back at her for never being nice. To her face, though, I have to call her grandmother. Penny simply calls her GG for now, though, I'm sure that'll have to change soon. Penny can do that many syllables; she just chooses not to.

With a simple nod, Penny heads back to my room while I head downstairs to start a load of laundry. Just as I close the door to the washer, I hear my name yelled. I leave the basket of clothes that will still need to be washed on the floor near the appliances as I head back towards the door.

"Hudson! There you are. Take my things down to my room," Judy orders as she removes her shoes. She pauses to look at me and visibly grimaces. Glad to know I look great today. She brought two whole suitcases for a night. Just what I need. To drag suitcases down stairs when I'm not even supposed to lift my daughter. These are definitely heavier than her.

"Is one of these presents that I should take them upstairs?" Might as well be strategic about the work I have to do.

"Just take them downstairs," she orders again. Fine then. Avoid my question.

I take the suitcases, identical in color – bright pink – and size – way too big for the fact that she's only staying one night - downstairs one at a time. This is the kind of suitcase you'd take to go to California for a whole week, maybe even bigger.

Once I drop them on the floor, relieved to let my ribs relax, I crack open the zipper of each. There's wrapped presents in one of them. With that knowledge, I go upstairs. Standing at the top of the stairs, I ask, "Are you sure you didn't want me to bring one of those bags up, Grandmother? It had presents." As I'm speaking, Penny glides up behind me, hiding behind my leg. "We can put them under the tree," I tell her.

"Were you trying to steal my things, boy? Probably hoping I have jewelry for you to pawn to pay for...that," she makes a hand motion toward Penny as though she isn't a human.

"First of all, Penny is my daughter and you will refer to her as such. Secondly, I was looking to see if there were presents for me to bring up because it's Christmas and you brought a ridiculous amount of baggage. I wouldn't steal, let alone from you. I don't need money to take care of my daughter. I work." In all honesty, my parents help pay for full time daycare. I'm sure she knows that, but it's another reason why I wouldn't have to steal. Even when she does wear jewelry, though, it isn't anything worth much money. It's big, gaudy jewelry made out of feathers or rocks. Jewelry you'd find at a craft show rather than the kind that you can pawn.

"You're a child. You shouldn't have a daughter," she sniffs.

"Well, it's a bit late for changing that now, isn't it?" I ask, picking up Penny. I know I'm not supposed to, but she needs me. She tucks her face into my shoulder. Rather than answering, my grandmother turns away from me. Rather than waiting for another sarcastic comment, I turn and carry Penny back to her room. I guess we're going to play with dolls until we're forced to come out.

*****

It isn't until my brother arrives around noon that we get called. If they hadn't called soon, we might have needed to slink out for a snack. I've mostly been laying on the floor while Penny plays. Part of me was tempted to curl up in her bed for a nap after last night being a late night and my head still hurting a little. Instead, I just lay on the floor thinking about what I learned from Piper last night. Tempted to know what my face looks like, I reach for my pocket to open snapchat. Except I don't have my phone. I don't have Piper on snapchat. This sucks. I just continue to lay on the floor, giving a last painful groan before dealing with people.

"Daddy," Penny whines, peeking out the door towards where all the people are. Right. Christmas. George. Grandmother.

"I'm coming," I answer. When I stand, I have to take a moment to simply move my legs and let the stiffness out of my muscles. I was still for too long. I'm not even 20 and I'm already this stiff. Probably not a good omen for the shape of my body in the future, let alone the prospect of ever playing at a higher level if this happens in high school. When there's feeling in my legs again, I head through the doorway to the living room, feeling my shadow following behind me.

When I reach the end of the hallway, I pause. There's a girl in the living room. Like, a girl other than my grandmother or mother. When she and my brother turn toward me, I see she's pretty. George has a girlfriend? Like, a serious enough girlfriend to take home for a holiday?

Past them, my mother appears to be panicking. Not only did she not set enough spots at the table for her, but none of us got presents for someone we didn't know existed. "Hey, George. Long time no see," I say, trying too hard to be casual. It has been a year since I've seen him, but he should've warned someone he was bringing a girl home.

When he looks up, he grimaces. "What happened to your face?"

"Sore subject," I answer, smiling a little at the double meaning. I lift up my shift a little to show the bruising on my ribs too, which just makes him make another face. "Anyways, good to see you," I say, taking the opportunity to pull him close in a half hug and ask, "A girl?"

George pushes me away while making it look like I just stepped away from him. He doesn't like when I comment on him not having girlfriends usually. "This is Rebecca," he introduces to the room in general. She has green eyes to contrast her dark hair and she looks around as George says all of our names. Well, everyone except Penny.

"Hi everyone," she starts, seemingly overwhelmed. Then she pauses and says, "I didn't know you have a little sister too." When she says that, she ducks down to look at Penny who must still be behind me.

George coughs before saying, "I don't."

"Do you have another sibling that this one belongs to then?" Okay, I'm already annoyed with her. I cross my arms, waiting for George to answer. He's looking at me like he doesn't want to. Like he doesn't want to admit that he thinks I've ruined my life.

"She's mine," I finally answer after too much silence. Turning, I reach back to hold Penny's hand which causes her to just hide up against my legs, not even peeking over at all the people. She's not usually this shy. It almost makes me think she can sense that she isn't necessarily wanted by most of the people here.

Rebecca, to her credit, has the decency to look embarrassed. Her face turns pink as she asks me, "What's her name?"

"Penelope," George finally says. He skipped her in the introductions after all.

Whether wanting to help with the tenseness or not, my grandmother says, "George, will you go down to my room and get the gifts? Your brother brought them all down there rather than under the tree up here." I have to roll my eyes. I offered and got accused of stealing her things to pawn.

While my brother heads downstairs, carrying a couple duffle bags with him, everyone looks back to Rebecca. She's thin and her hair is curled. She's wearing makeup and a dress. George and I obviously have different tastes in girls, because other than the dark hair, she doesn't look like Piper at all. Piper is bigger and her eyes are dark. This girl's nose is thinner and her cheeks aren't as round. Something about her gives off the vibes that she might be smart. She'd probably have to be for George to spend any time with her. Maybe it's just how she holds herself, tall and confident. Rather than avert her gaze like most of my family, she watches Penny and I like she's curious. He must not have told her much about our family. Not only did she not know about Penny, but he said his relation to each of us with our names. I can almost guarantee she's trying to figure out how old I am. How old Penny is. She isn't going to guess right. No one does. Everyone ages me up once they know Penny exists and they pretty much always age her down, despite her talking pretty well.

"So, what are you majoring in?" she asks me, guessing wrong.

"I'm in high school," I say bluntly, not offering her much to work with.

"Oh," she answers, surprised. "Are you a senior this year?" I nod, and she continues. "So what are you going to do next year?" she putting in more effort than George usually does, and she's actually asking what I'm doing rather than assuming.

"Not sure yet, maybe I'll go to college, play hockey." When I see the judgemental looks on my parents' faces, I add, "Maybe I'll just work for a while."

"You know who else was a teen dad?" she asks, looking eager to share her knowledge.

"LeBron? He was almost 20 when his son was born." I've heard that one and it's not too pertinent when he was already a pro athlete.

"Lil Wayne was 15 when his daughter was born, though, and he had a successful career after that."

"Hadn't he already dropped out of school to focus on music anyways?" I'm pretty sure that one was on a click bait article I read.

"Maybe," she answers, shrugging. "What about Vince Neil? You know, the singer of Mötley Crüe."

"What about him?"

"His first kid was born when he was 17." Why does Rebecca know so many celebrities who were teen parents? It seems like a niche part of trivia to know unless you've specifically looked it up.

I don't know too much about this one, but I can guess. "Being a rock star, he probably was never around, though. She already doesn't know her mom, she's not getting a complete absentee father, too."

"Better to not be around when they're little than once they'll remember," Rebecca answers with a shrug. She's so nonchalant about it, I can't tell if she knows from experience or not, but I think I like her. She's talked to me more since I've met her than George has in the last couple of years.

*****

On Sunday, I'm working a cashiering shift. Usually we'd be pulling ad items from this week and stocking for next week, but now stockers are down one. On the bright side, it seems like extra people are doing Sunday shopping today before the week ahead, so it's a good thing I'm here.

I made sure to take a few ibuprofen before I started, because I had a bad feeling about the moving in general. Turns out, I was right. Twisting from the right to grab the items the customers put on the belt, scanning it, and then twisting to the left to put it on the belt for them to pack up is not great on the ribs. It's definitely better than lifting cans and pasta boxes and who knows what else, though. With my luck, there would've been a bunch of Gatorade or pop that needed to be stocked.

Around noon, I look up as I'm scanning items to see a familiar face walking past the checkout aisles. Piper is here with a cart full of groceries. She didn't see me though, all she saw was the person with a full cart still loading on my belt. I try to follow where she goes as I'm scanning, but lose track of her. I need to pay attention to my own customer. After a couple minutes, I feel like I'm being watched.

When I look up again, she's about two aisles in front of me, waiting to pay at her aisle, looking straight at me. As soon as she sees me looking, she looks away. She laughs at something that cashier says. Damn Kristian. He better not be trying to steal my girl...she is my girl, right?

I go on scanning, trying to catch Piper's eye as she's packing her groceries. Is she avoiding looking at me? Do I look that bad with the black eye? Is she going to refuse to talk to me after the thing with her dad?

"Run into a door?"

"What?" I ask, looking at the man in front of me as I scan the last item. He must be sixty years old, but he's laughing.

"Your eye. Did you run into a door or something?"

"Oh, something like that," I answer, smiling. I tell him his total after double checking there's nothing under his cart. After he pays, I find Piper looking at me as she puts her last bag in her cart. She gives me a tiny smile and mouths something to me as she starts walking, past my till and out the door.

I have to replay it a couple times in my head. What did she say? All I can come up with is, "Nice tie." I have to look down and see what I'm wearing. Everyone who works here has to wear black pants, a button up shirt, and a tie to go with the black aprons. The ties are where we get our individuality. My tie is blue with hockey sticks all over it. When we got it when I was in ninth grade, my mom said that this blue brought out my eyes. It was when she occasionally said nice things to me without much thought.

Seeing Piper here when I'm working, I can't help but think that I want more from my life than working at the grocery store. I love it and the people are great. Some people are happy with it, but I want more. Scouts talk to me a lot. Maybe I could go play somewhere and go to college. Maybe even somewhere that will give me a scholarship.

16

When I get to school Monday, I'm exhausted. To add to my injuries and having to deal with my family, Penny has an ear infection. She was irritable by the time I got home from work yesterday. We tried to do dinner, bath time, and bed like usual, but she wasn't sleeping and was running a fever. Of course, it looked fantastic when I brought her to the ER at 11 at night and I walked in, unable to carry her and with a black eye. Naturally, it looked even better when we had the same doctor as I had on Friday. I only got a couple hours of sleep by the time I got her home and we had her fever down so she could sleep. This morning was a fight to take antibiotics and some ibuprofen to go to daycare. My parents are still mad at me and figure this is an even better punishment for my irresponsibility, so they aren't helping me with any of it.

I just want a few minutes of peace, so I grab the book I brought home from Piper's house and head to class. It's a few minutes later than her usual when Piper comes through the door, looking at me strangely. I'm tired. I'm crabby after my parents left everything to me when they know I didn't sleep well the last couple nights. She goes to her desk, setting her books down and looks at me. After she sits down, she whispers, "Hey."

I repeat the word back without looking up. My hair is even tired. It's not staying back like it usually does. It's falling in my face, but I'm just letting since it hides my black eye. It really has gone from a little bit of redness initially to a true shiner now.

"How'd it go over the weekend?" Piper asks.

"Not great." I can sense her getting frustrated with my short answers, but I don't want to talk. To add to how I look, my head still hurts a little and my ribs somehow seem to be getting more sore. Since I'm not talking, Piper turns forward and opens the book that's on top of her stack of school supplies. It's what she brings to every class. Textbook for the class, folder to put any worksheets in, notebook to take notes, a mechanical pencil, and whatever book she happens to be reading. The one she has today is called Geekerella and wasn't on her bookshelf this weekend - at least, not that I remember.

Next thing I know, Leo has shown up to class and starts talking. "Dude, I've barely heard from you since the game the other day. You only sent me one text and then didn't text me back. I started to question if you were alive. So, how you doing, man?" With the last sentence, he slaps my back. Trying not to be too dramatic, I only let out a cough, but I reach for my ribs anyways.

"Watch the ribs, asshole. Maybe you didn't hear from me because I don't have a phone now," I say, finally closing the book and looking up at him.

"Holy shit, your face. And what do you mean you don't have a phone?"

With that, practically everyone in the room, including Piper, turns to look at me. Great. Some of the girls are holding their hands to their mouths. The guys I don't get along with as well almost look like they're enjoying that my face doesn't look great, probably figuring it gives them a better chance with the girls. Looking over at Piper, she looks sad, looking at my face. Naturally, I look back down at the book, pretending I don't notice. When I glance back up at her, though, she's turned around reading her book again.

"My phone got taken away. My mom was pissed that I stayed out so late Friday night after all that. Then, she was even more mad at the fact that I didn't warn her I wasn't coming home at all and didn't see me until Saturday morning. You missed asking about my ribs," I point out, trying to distract Leo from the fact that I said I didn't go home.

"Your ribs are fine enough if you're here sitting in a desk," Leo says simply, raising his hand like he's going to hit me on the back again. He means it to be friendly, but right now my ribs don't see it that way. Instead, I lean to try to avoid him, and instead make my ribs hurt anyways. "Don't worry, I won't actually hit you." Leo starts laughing, hardly able to control himself as he collapses backwards into his own seat. "Now where were you that you didn't go home? I don't think the hospital was that busy. And I can't imagine that you felt that good..." Leo trails off.

When Leo trails off, I look over to find him looking toward Piper. I can tell even from the back that her face is turning red. "Maybe you did…" Leo starts. I have to think fast to keep him from embarrassing Piper even more, so I grab the book I borrowed from Piper and hit his arm. "Ouch! You hit me with a book!" he nearly shouts, rubbing his arm where I hit it. Meanwhile, I double over as the effort of moving my arm to hit Leo shoots down into my ribs.

"Mr. Melville and Mr. Scott. Please, try to control yourselves and keep it down," Mrs. Johnson scolds from the front of the room. She's sitting at her desk in the front corner of the room before she takes attendance.

"Did you actually hurt your ribs?" Leo finally asks me as an afterthought.

"The doctor said I just bruised them, but yes. I also have a minor concussion and potentially broke my nose."

"I think it's safe to say your nose is broken and you have a very pretty black eye as well," Leo cackles. I hold up my book in a threat to hit him, and he quickly stops.

"Do you want one to match?"

"Boys," Mrs. Johnson scolds sharply. "Do I need to separate you? You're disrupting your classmates. Mr. Melville, I appreciate seeing you reading, now put your nose back in the book instead of using it to abuse others. Books are not for hitting. That's something I tell my two-year-old grandson. I shouldn't have to tell a teenage boy. Mr. Scott, you could take a lesson from your friend and pick up a book. Or even better, read the one that's assigned to you."

Everyone in class is delighted by the burn and ohhhhhhhs. One boy even yelled that Leo might need some cream for that burn. The redheaded woman standing in the aisle between Leo and I looks between us. "Are we ready for attendance now, boys?"

"Yes, ma'am," I answer quietly. Putting the book back down in front of me before cracking it open.

"I guess," Leo agrees, slumping in his chair.

She smiles at each of us before turning around and walking back to the front of the room, grabbing the piece of paper to read names off of. When I look forward to Piper, she's smiling, looking up to Mrs. Johnson.

*****

In accounting, my spot is almost all the way in the back. The spot behind me used to be empty, but now Piper is filling it. At the beginning of class, Ms. Mayhew hands out a packet to keep us busy for at least part of the class period. It's a simple one, she tells us. A list of expenses with their dates and amounts, as well as revenue. It also states that there's some accounts payable entries that need to be paid off since the last week. We just need to put all of these into the ledger.

Ms. Mayhew drops five packets at the front of each row that each person has to hand to the person behind them. It takes a few minutes since teenagers are horrible at paying attention enough to actually hand things back like they're supposed to. When I get two packets, I put one down on the desk before turning around with Piper's. She holds out her hand for it, but I pause as I'm putting it in her hand.

"What?" I ask.

"Was everything okay at home the other night after you got home?" It kept eating at me that she was sneaking around in her house so her dad didn't realize I was there. He didn't seem happy at the hospital.

"I'm fine," she replies, taking her packet from my hand.

"Are you sure?"

"Yes. Do your work and worry about yourself. Obviously, you have a lot more to worry about," she answers shortly. Setting the packet on her desk, she uses her left hand to block her paper. She grabs her mechanical pencil and starts writing quickly. As I watch her, she flips her pencil around to erase several lines. Looking up, she says, "Please, do your own work and don't copy off of me."

"I wasn't going to copy. I was just making sure you were okay," I mumble as I turn around and look at the paper. She's done in less than 10 minutes and races to the front to turn it in first. When she turns around, she nearly trips over her oversized boots. When she collapses back in her seat, I hear fidgeting until the sound of pages being flipped stops and there's silence. She's reading.

17

It's been a few days since the fight. Penny is sleeping again with her ear infection clearing, thank God. Piper and I are talking again, at least more than that first day, but I think that was more my fault of being too tired to try at all after bringing Penny to the ER the night before. I went to practice the last couple of days, but today coach told me not to bother. All I can do right now is watch, and he knows I have other things I need to do, by which I'm sure he meant taking care of Penny. Today, though, I didn't tell my mother that I don't have to go to practice. Penny is at daycare, and I'm going to try to make things right with Piper.

First, I drive by her work. Her car isn't there. Next, I go to her house. When I get close, though, I notice that Piper's car isn't in the driveway, but a truck is. It must be her dad's truck because it wasn't there when we got there the other night, but it was when we left in the morning. Where is she? I reach toward my cupholder before remembering that I don't have my phone. I wonder how long my parents are going to keep up the no phone thing since that also means they can't contact me. I even had to find my watch so I'll know what time it is.

Whipping a u-turn, I go back the way I came. As I'm driving down the road, I notice the giant deer statue. In the parking lot just past it, there's a car that looks like it could be Piper's. At the next road, I take a left to find the entrance to the parking lot. Parking next to the car, I get out before looking around. I nearly think she isn't there, until I notice her on top of a piece of playground equipment. She's wearing jeans, a black hoodie, and a grey hat. When I start walking toward her, I expect her to look up, but she doesn't I'm practically standing under the equipment she's laying on top of while reading before I finally say, "You really should be more aware of your surroundings." With that, she finally looks down at me, looking surprised to see me.

"I heard a car. I heard the car door. I just didn't feel like looking up because I assumed it was little kids here to run off energy." She shrugs before looking back at the book. Trying to look at the cover, I find the title. Geekerella still. Kinda seems like it'd describe her, a bit of a geek, but also, really pretty.

"So, you were just planning to hog the playground equipment then?"

"Maybe," she answers, smiling. She doesn't look back down at me, though. She's looking at the book, but I can tell she isn't actually reading it.

"Are you really going to keep ignoring me when I drove 20 minutes here to see you? And I had to find you when you weren't at your house and I don't have a phone?" I ask, feeling like I might as well just go pick up Penny if she isn't going to talk to me.

"I suppose not. Why are you here?" she asks, finally closing her book.

"I'm sorry," I say simply, stuffing my hands in my jeans pockets.

"For what?" she asks. She sounds like she genuinely doesn't know.

"Ignoring you for me getting grounded when you did what I asked."

"So, you're not sorry about the fight itself?"

"Not particularly. I'm also not sorry about making sure you were okay. I'm not sure if that also made you mad."

"I mean, it annoyed me. I really am okay. It's not like he hits me or anything. More...he ignores me. That night at the hospital was the most we've talked since I got him to agree to switching schools and we went in and did the paperwork."

"God, Piper." I can't help but shake my hand. This is how she lives?

"I'm just fine. It's only since my mom died. I think I remind him of her and that she's gone..." She blinks up at the sky like she's trying to keep from crying.

Reaching up between the monkey bars she's on top of, I hold her hand and ask, "Will you please come down here so I can give you a hug?" Nodding, she blinks again and I see a tear rolling down her cheek. She hands me her book as she begins the climb down.

When she's on the second to the bottom rung, she turns around. I'm standing at the bottom waiting, but she holds out her arms. When I step closer, she throws her arms around my neck, hugging me. Wrapping my arms around her, I pull her down to ground level and she tucks her face into my navy blue sweater.

"How do you wear that sweater and look so damn good? Most guys probably couldn't pull it off."

"I look good in anything I put on this body," I say, trying to make her laugh. I can't help but laugh at that one myself. Her arms tighten around me before she looks up, smiling. When I smile back down at her, I wipe the tears from her cheeks.

Dropping her forehead back onto my chest, she asks, "Did you really come all this way just to apologize?"

Resting my chin on the top of her head, I say, "Yeah, it's not like I could call or text without a phone. Plus, I figured this way I might get to spend a few minutes with you." I kiss the top of her head before just resting my head there.

"What did you want to do?"

"What's with the deer?" I ask, nodding toward the statue. It's facing the road. "I saw it when we drove to your house last week." I've seen it before, but never paid it much attention before.

"I'm not sure when it was first put there, but I'm pretty sure it's been there our whole lives. Like 10 years ago it was painted to be the world's largest white stag. I liked to pretend it was Harry Potter's patronus. They painted it back the next year, though. There are a few other identical ones around the state and in surrounding states, all painted a little different. None of them are all white, though."

An idea pops into my head and, before I can shoo it away, I take Piper's hand and say, "C'mon." Realizing the book is still in my hand, I pause, dropping her hand, and jog over to my truck. Dropping it in the passenger seat, I slam the door shut and jog back to her. Jogging is definitely painful, but it's gotten slightly better even in the last couple days. If anything, I've gotten good at either figuring out what not to do, or pretending it's not hurting. Piper gives me a quizzical look when I return to her, so I explain, "I thought I'd leave your book in there so I don't have to carry it with us."

We have to sludge through 8 inches of snow for about 200 feet before we get to the giant deer and of course I'm just wearing my tennis shoes. Snow keeps falling between my socks and shoes. I might get frost bite from the snow sitting against my feet. When I look back at Piper following me, I find that she's using my footprints. Because so she's so much shorter than me, though, she's practically hopping from track to track. Deciding to take it easy on her, I try to take smaller steps so she can walk a little more normally.

When we reach the deer, I pause to look up at it. "Have you ever climbed it?"

"I have a picture sitting on its back from when I was, like, 4. My dad is behind me though, standing on those logs it's jumping over, so I'm guessing he probably set me up there."

"Let's try to get up there!" A better memory for her of this deer.

"You're going to hurt yourself again," she answers, looking between me, the deer, and then the ground.

"I'll be fine. I want to sit up there." On the side we're standing on, the log the deer is jumping over is split into two pieces versus the other side being one big log. I step onto the platform which gives me a couple more inches before I put a foot up onto the lower log.

"You're only wearing tennies? Aren't your feet wet and cold?" Piper asks, forgetting to be concerned about me getting hurt.

"I wasn't expecting to be hanging out in the snow when I came to find you. I assumed you'd be home when you weren't at work," I shrug.

With a little climbing that I probably shouldn't be doing, I manage to stand on the lower log. Then, I put my left foot up on the second log which doesn't have much of a lip at all. When I look at the deer now, it's back is just past waist height. Finally, Piper says, "You know my legs are shorter and I'm shorter. This isn't going to work the same for me." Looking down at her, I realize that she's now eye level with my feet. She is short.

"First of all, there was a step onto a pedestal to help before I stepped up on to the log. My legs aren't that long either. Second of all, you have me to help you." If I sound confident, she'll feel more confident.

"I don't think you're technically supposed to climb it."

"I don't care what we're technically supposed to do. I technically would really like to kiss you, but I'm doing this instead because it seems like it'll get me in less trouble than kissing you has so far."

I'm not sure what I was expecting her reaction to be, but she laughs. "Those shoes at least have good tread on them, right?" She pokes my shoes, making me wiggle my toes.

"I'm not going to fall." Sound confident. Putting a leg up like I'm mounting a horse, I pause and put it back down. Still a little high.

"Can't do it?" Piper teases. Rather than answering, I use my arms to push myself higher. From that position, I can swing my leg up easily to be straddling the deer.

Throwing her hands up in the air, Piper asks, "Now what do I do?"

Trying to act like it's obvious, I say, "Do what I did."

"Because it's that simple. You're a freaking giant." Cracking a grin, I nearly make an inappropriate comment, but close my eyes and focus on keeping my balance and not annoying her.

"C'mon. A step up next to the logs is the first step." Piper nods and follows my instructions. From there, though, she stops and looks around like she's going to get arrested for climbing the statue. It's starting to get dark already since it's deep winter, so we won't be as visible.

"Do you want my hand or do you want to try yourself first?" I ask, holding out my hand to her as I'm straddling the deer so I at least have a little extra balance. She looks between my hand and the log, putting her hands on the top log for balance, while attempting to reach her foot up onto the bottom log.

Within 30 seconds she declares, "I can't do it, my foot can't reach up there. My legs just aren't long enough." She stares at me expectantly, like I'm going to get down.

Instead, I decide to be difficult. Bending forward and reaching out my hand, I tell her, "Give me your left hand." When she does, I add my second instruction. "Put your right hand on the top log." She does as I say, but looks confused at what's going to happen. "Push up with your right hand on the log and then once you get a little more height, then put your right foot up on the other one." She opens her mouth to argue, but instead closes it. Doing what I said, she only gains a couple inches, so I start to lean back, pulling her up. It seems to take her a second to realize what I'm doing, but when she does, she quickly pulls a foot onto the log.

When both feet are on the log, she quickly steps her right foot up to the second log. She does that one without issue, but I keep hold of a hand to give her more balance than just the side of the deer. There, she pauses again.

"If I fall and hurt myself, it's your fault and you get to deal with me like I dealt with you. Except, that wasn't my fault, so I'm not sure how I ended up with you. My health insurance card is in my wallet. My wallet is in my purse which is in the trunk of my car. My keys are in the front pocket of my sweatshirt. Please don't go to my house and tell my dad before you take me to the hospital. I'd rather go with you." That seems a little bit extreme, but to ease her mind, I just nod my agreement.

Letting go of my hand, she reaches both arms over the deer's back. First, she doesn't seem to move, but I realize she's testing her weight on it before she switches which foot her weight is on. Relaxing, she takes a deep breath and stares at the deer. As she's focused, I spin around to face where she's about to come up here before I back up further to be between the deer's shoulder blades.

"Think you can do that with a little more pulling your body up to get your leg up?" I ask, trying to encourage her.

"No way," she says simply.

Sighing as dramatically as I can, I simply look down at her. A few pieces of hair are falling into my face, right over the bruised eye and I push them back with my hand. "You really want to test how healed my ribs are already, don't you?"

"I really don't. I'm just not strong and am only doing this because you're peer pressuring me."

"Oh, I'm peer pressuring you, am I?"

"You are," she answers, smiling up at me. If I were really peer pressuring her into something she didn't want to do, I don't think she'd be smiling at me like that.

"Put your arms around the deer and pull with all your strength," I say, knowing I need to change the subject. That little smile might be the death of me. When she does as I instructed, I reach my hands out and start pulling by her armpits. My ribs are screaming as I pull. Leaning forward is already iffy, let alone then trying to pull. If I'm not supposed to play hockey or lift Penny, I sure as hell am not supposed to do this, but it might be memorable for her. I want to be memorable.

"You're going to hurt yourself," she grunts. I know she's putting in effort, but I'm not sure if she's doing most of the effort, or if I am.

"Just keep pulling," I say through my teeth. She's high enough now that with a quick movement, she can reach out an arm to be further over the deer and give herself more traction. It only takes maybe a minute to fully get her on the deer. When she's almost flat, she is able to swing a leg to the other side of it so she's straddling it's back. Breathing hard, she simply lays there for a minute before she sits up. With her safely up here, I lean back against the deer's neck, holding my ribs. Maybe I should take it easy like the doctor said. I could've dropped her if I bent wrong and something hurt more than it already did.

"I made it!" she grins finally, throwing her hands up in the air like she just won an award rather than making it to the top of a statue with my help.

Sitting up and still holding my hand against my ribs, I ask, "Does it count as you making it up here when I did that much work?"

"Hey!" She almost sounds offended, but by the joking tone in her voice, I can also tell she recognizes it's true. Then, noting my hand against my stomach, her face changes to one of worry and she says, "I'm sorry. Did you hurt yourself? Did I hurt you? Are you okay?" She scoots forward on the deer to be closer to me, reaching out her hand toward where I hurt like she'll be able to magically fix it by touching the area.

"I'm okay, that was just a lot of physical activity for someone who isn't at hockey because of my ribs. It was worth it to see you that excited." When she is still frowning, I poke the spot on her cheek where there was a dimple when she was smiling.

When Piper's face starts to turn red, she backs up on the deer again. "Hey, come back here," I say, reaching out for her. She reaches out a hand toward me, so I gently tug on it until she shimmies back toward me. Then, out of nowhere, she reaches out a hand to push my hair out of my face.

"What do you look like with shorter hair?"

"Wouldn't you like to know?" I say, grinning playfully, but also thinking, horrified, about when my hair was last short.

"I would like to know. Got any pictures?"

"Considering I don't have my phone, I don't. Also, any of those pictures are at least three years old and I'd rather not show anyone. Little pizza face hadn't grown into himself yet. You were cute as a kid. If you saw a picture of me, you'd run away."

"There's a reason I don't have pictures from the last few years either. Aren't the early teen years the worst for everyone?"

"I guess." Thinking of some of those preteens I see strutting around school, I grimace. "Though, even the younger kids at our school are starting to look way too grown up in those awkward years. They need to suffer too. I swear, I'm going to make sure Penny doesn't even get makeup until she's 15, at least."

"Ouch. So, I should go buy her some makeup with my next paycheck?"

Throwing a hand to my chest like she just stabbed me, I say, "You wound me! My girlfriend! Going against my direct wishes!"

"Guess that's what you risk when you let someone into her life. You should've known when you saw how I was with the treats for the game last week."

"You're not wrong," I answer, giving a small shrug. I also wouldn't have given her that many snacks or any specific instructions if there wasn't going to be a person who could actually read. Moving a little bit forward, our knees bump. We can't sit any closer unless we're overlapping somehow. Whispering, I say, "I really like you being in both of our lives." When I lean a little closer, Piper does too. I don't think she even notices she does. Resting my hand on her cheek, I finish leaning forward for a kiss.

When she leans her forehead against mine, eyes closed, I know she must have forgiven me. "I like it, too, but did you mean it when you just called me your girlfriend?"

"If you're okay with that. I kind of thought with how the last couple weeks have been, it's kinda become implied."

"I'm okay with it." she smiles, just about a grin, but I can tell she's trying to hold back her excitement just a little. Suddenly, with a glint in her eye she asks, "Wait, Facebook? Instagram?"

"What are you talking about?" Mentally, I try to rewind our conversation in my head. Pictures of me with short hair. "Please don't. I'd rather you not creep through my profile to see younger me. Plus, I always feel guilty on social media that the posts I have have no sign of Penny, so I barely post." Really, I only post a few times a year and most of it is just sharing other people's posts, usually hockey stuff.

"Fine..." she answers, putting out a lip in a pout and leaning towards me until her head is pressed against my shoulder.

"Wow, you're milking it. Good thing I have practice saying no to a pouty face."

"You kinda suck," she answers in a normal voice again, picking up her head to kiss my cheek.

"Too bad you don't." I couldn't stop the comment from coming out. I didn't even think it before it came out of my mouth. She simply stares at me, surprised. She'd probably expect that from a lot of guys, but not me. I haven't said anything like that around her. "Wait, shit. I did not mean to say that out loud. Okay, for that, I'll let you follow me or friend me or whatever. I'm still going to *beg* you not to look at pictures more than two years old."

"Penny is older than that."

"You're not wrong." What does that have to do with anything? I already told her I don't have pictures of Penny on there.

"You couldn't have looked that bad, then." Ahh, there it is.

"Not compared to my classmates, anyways," I answer, feeling like I need a smart ass comment. Most boys that age have acne. That much didn't scare away the girls.

Piper puts her hand over her mouth, trying to hold back giggles. I barely hear an "Ouch" as she sits back and finally lets the giggles bubble over.

18

Last night, Piper and I fell asleep on the phone. We were GroupWatching a movie on Disney + that she said she loved. As much as she had tried to convince me to watch one of the High School Musicals, I didn't cave. Instead, we watched that Rapunzel movie since Penny was still half awake in my bed with me. Since it was Friday night, I just let her go to sleep in my bed since it meant me sleeping in my own bed too. We've been taking turns finding movies to watch each night. Apparently she's the type of person to talk though a movie, making sarcastic comments, singing along, whatever comes to her mind. It drives me crazy when Leo does it, but it's actually kind of endearing when Piper does it.

I've waited long enough. I was waiting to text her so that I don't wake her up, but it's almost 10. I can't wait any longer. I convinced my parents I need my phone back when I'm driving to and from school and transporting Penny all the time. "What are you up to today?" I send, after debating at least three different ways of phrasing it. Do I bring up her birthday now or surprise her?

"Not much. I was thinking about going to the library." I get in reply.

"Mind if we come over?"

"We?"

"P and I." Who else would 'we' be?

"Sure?" I'm not sure what to think of the question mark, but I'll ignore it. It's probably because I haven't acknowledged her birthday yet or really opted to come to her house, let alone with Penny. On the drive over, we make a quick stop at the grocery store. Penny is just old enough to understand that birthdays are exciting and mean cake and presents which makes her my perfect companion today.

On arrival, Piper's car is the only one in the driveway. Her dad isn't home with her on her birthday? Now I feel bad for waiting so long to text her. I guess I understand why she was just going to go to the library. I help Penny out and hold her hand as we walk up to the door. Knocking, I ensure the bag with what we picked up is tucked behind me. When she answers the door, she looks cute. Her hair is down and wavy as it looks like it's still partially wet. She's wearing jeans and a cute, green sweater that's really flattering on her.

As soon as the door is open enough for Penny to fit through, she runs through, yelling, "Happy birfday!" as she goes for a hug from Piper. When Piper picks her up, squeezing her through her winter jacket to hug her, I almost feel bad. By the look on her face, I can tell she just needed to hear those words from someone that cared.

"I did say it last night on the phone, but happy birthday," I say, leaning forward to kiss the beautiful girl in front of me. When my hand touches her arm for balance, I note that not only is her sweater flattering, but it's soft too.

"I don't think it counts when it wasn't midnight yet," she points out, gently setting Penny back on the floor. She's not wrong. I was probably before 11 when we both fell asleep last night. "What are you holding?" she asks, noting my arm still behind my back.

"A present."

Blinking quickly, she asks, "Really?"

Did I do something wrong? "What is it?"

"I didn't get any last year. I wasn't really expecting to this year either."

"Well, now I need to give you a hug, just in case you don't like it. It's kind of, create your own present, if we're being honest." I'm just trying to hedge my bets with a hug cheering her up, but she does seem to relax into my hugs most of the time. With that, I scoop her up in a big hug that pulls her feet off the ground as she throws her arms around my neck. We pull away about an inch and there's a pause long enough that my mouth almost speaks before my brain gives it permission, but instead I give her another kiss. My mouth can't betray me with words if I'm kissing her.

When we pull apart, I tell her to close her eyes. She follows directions and holds out her hands. When I plop the box into them, her fingers close around it, but hesitate. She moves her arms up and down with her eyes still closed, testing the weight of the object. "Am I allowed to look at what it is?"

When Penny answers in the affirmative, she finds a box of marble cake mix in her hands.

"Did you get frosting too?" Should I have? Is this a bad idea?

"Ummm, so that's part of it. I remembered the picture of you and your mom. I thought maybe we could make our own frosting for it." What if she doesn't have the ingredients? I shouldn't have assumed. This was stupid.

"That's what we did every year. We made a cake together and decorated it with homemade frosting."

"Is that okay?" She nods, so I somewhat change the subject to give her a second, "Penny, let's get our jackets and boots off."

As we take off our boots and I hang our jackets on the coat tree by the door, Piper takes an old, white mixer from one of the lower cupboards. Next, she grabs a step stool and puts it in front of the stove. From the cupboard above the stove, she comes down with a recipe book. Upon opening it, I see it's a book of recipe cards. The card she takes out, though, isn't on one of the slots - it's just tucked into the front cover.

When I move closer to look, I see the ingredients written in half-cursive: crisco, powdered sugar, almond extract, egg white, a dash of salt. You can see the splatters of frosting and powdered sugar that have gotten all over it. "This is my favorite recipe. My grandma's. It's her mixer too. Frosting is the only thing we - I - use it for anymore."

Piper directs us toward the spice cupboard to find the vegetable oil, sticks of crisco and full bag of powdered sugar along with the almond extract as she grabs the eggs out of the fridge and starts the oven preheating for the cake. Two separate bowls are required for the making of marble cake. The larger white one goes to us, and Piper keeps the smaller clear bowl as she steals the chocolate mix to her side of the counter. While waiting for us to mix the vanilla mix, she starts making faces. "Am I doing something wrong?" I ask, pretty sure I'm not, but feeling unsure with the face she's making.

"Well, Penny might be better at cracking eggs than you because this is going to be some crunchy cake if you don't get those pieces of shells out!" She laughs as I look down, trying to pick pieces of shells from the bowl in front of me.

Instead, of just watching me and waiting, she gets another small bowl out of the cupboard. In a quick movement, she cracks an egg against the counter once, before she moves it above the bowl, pushes her thumbs where it's cracked to split the shell into two mostly even halves, and starts tipping the yolk back and forth between the two halves to let all the white fall into the bowl underneath. When it's only yolk left in the egg shelf and she turns to throw the egg away, she finds Penny and I both watching her. Quickly, I pick up the whisk to start trying to meld it all together. When there's no more lumps, Piper takes a measuring cup to steal some of our mix.

"Hey! That mines!" Penny exclaims at Piper.

"I use your vanilla to make my chocolate. See?" She says, dumping the mix into her small bowl that she had already poured the chocolate powder into and starting to whisk them together. There's something satisfying about watching the cake mix turn from white to chocolate and Penny must agree, because she just stands on the step stool and watches.

I'm directed to use the partial crisco to grease the pan as Piper finishes mixing. The white goes in first, and then we swirl in the chocolate, using a butter knife to make sure it's swirled throughout.

As soon as that's in the oven, we start on the frosting. A whole bag of powdered sugar goes in first so all the ingredients can go on top and maybe we can limit the sugar getting all over. Crisco, water, vanilla extract, and the egg white. "One thing I love about this mixer, is the timer. I can set it for a minute, and it'll stop after that. New mixers don't have that function," Piper explains. She sets it and then has to urge it to start turning, but once it does, it's happy to keep doing so. Even with the powdered sugar at the bottom, some of it flies into the air with the movement of the beaters. Without doing so from the prompt of the recipe, she grabs a spatula to scrape the thick mixture from the sides and pushes it toward the middle to allow it to be mixed in. After one minute, it beeps and stops.

"Now, ten minutes on speed ten." Penny's eyes go wide, seeming to understand that this is going to be fast. Piper sets it, and as it starts spinning, Penny makes an excited noise at the speed its going. Little splatters of frosting start flying and hit the bread box, the wall, and the counter. Penny is entranced by the mixer, so Piper uses it as an opportunity to throw dishes in the sink, clean up the garbage, and put ingredients away.

Piper pauses the mixer to scrape the sides, making sure everything is getting mixed in and pushes the frosting out of the beater blades. When I press start, Penny jumps up and down with the excitement of the speed and as I watch, the beaters get clogged up with the thick frosting again.

The frosting is done before the cake. Piper picks Penny up to sit on the counter, urging her to dip a finger in the bowl to taste test. Her eyes wide, she exclaims, "Yummy, yummy, yummy!" with a side to side dance that she does most times she gets something sweet.

Piper grabs some on her finger and puts it in her mouth, closing her eyes as though she can't take in the taste and anything visual at the same time. When she opens her eyes, I realize we're both watching her, waiting for a reaction.

"It passes the test," she says, dipping both her index fingers into the bowl. Even if she's going for another taste, why is she using both hands? "So thank you-" she says, tapping me on the nose with one of her frosting fingers "and thank you-" tapping Penny with the other "for coming and making it with me. She licks the remaining frosting off her fingers and looks between the two of us with our white noses. Pulling out her phone, she grins and says, "Now I need a picture of that. Maybe it can go next to the one of me and my mom."

I let her get a picture of the two of us before I grab some frosting with my finger to make her match us. "Now we need a picture of all three of us and that will be even better to put up." So, with Penny sitting on the counter and Piper and I on either side of her, we get a selfie of us with frosting on our noses, all cheesing for the camera.

19

Do I wear a shirt and tie? I've met Coach Maddox before. He came to my game the day Piper and I first met and talked to me for a couple minutes after the game. Then, I wasn't sure. Even last week, I wasn't sure I'd be able to make it work. Really, though, it could work. I think.

I finally pick a grey polo shirt and khaki pants. Coach gave me the option of where to eat, and I'm sure he was expecting somewhere fancy, but we're going to the McDonald's with the play place. If I'm going to play in college, I'm going to own my life. Penny is coming with to meet Coach. He needs to know the full me if he's potentially going to want me to play for his team, or maybe even give me a scholarship. A scholarship would be amazing.

Penny wanders into my room and looks even better than I do in her long-sleeved red dress with tiny flowers all over it. Paired with the pigtail braids that I finally figured out, she looks like she could be in Little House on the Prairie. She twirls around in her dress, since how much it spins is the best way to test how much she likes the dress, and grins at me.

"I think you need some leggings under that dress if you're going to play, Monkey."

She twirls again, seeing how far out she can make the skirts billow. After about four full spins, she stops, trying to figure out how to walk straight. Before she can collapse sideways into my desk, I scoop her up under her armpits. "No, daddy! Spin me!"

"We aren't going to spin anymore. We're going to find you leggings so we can go get lunch." Carrying her into her room, I drop her on her bed and pull open a drawer. It's amazing how easy it is to find the clothes you need when a lack of going to practice results in actually keeping up on laundry. She is mostly agreeable to putting them on and does so without too much argument. A pair of socks later, we're heading toward the door. Boots on for her. Dress shoes on my feet. Her hat and jacket on. My jacket in my arms to at least have in the truck in case it breaks down. Sometimes, I don't think it's even worth putting her jacket on when we just have to take it off again at the car seat, but when it's -20 degrees outside, it's worth it even for the run to the truck for her.

I already started the truck, so it's nice and warm for us. I practically toss Penny into her car seat, jacket still on, before I close the door and go around to my side. Once I'm inside with the doors closed, I strip her jacket off and get her buckled in. We're off.

When we get to McDonald's, Penny tries to run straight for the back door to the play place. I catch her by her hood, nearly causing her jacket to come off. Before that can happen, though, I manage to grab her hand.

"You need to wait until we get our food so that I can watch you. I can't watch you from here." Then, under my breath, I add, "I also need to find Coach."

I scan the room and find a man in his mid-thirties who could be my guy. I know I met him once, but I honestly wasn't paying that much attention. I didn't expect to need to recognize him later. He's wearing a maroon polo shirt and leaning against a divider between the ordering area and the seating area, looking around as though he's waiting for someone. I take a deep breath to mentally splint my ribs, and lift Penny to carry her with me.

Approaching the man, I ask, "Coach Maddox?"

"Yes? You're Hudson?"

"Yes, sir." I nod, holding out my right hand to shake his.

"I thought that might be you, but the little girl threw me off. Is this your sister? We could've rescheduled if you needed to babysit." Well, nothing like jumping right into it.

"Actually, sir, this is my daughter." First, he looks stricken. Then, his eyes start flicking between us. I can see him doing the mental math. I should put him out of his misery. "She's almost four, but I'm almost 19." Like that helps. "I plan to pay for her lunch. I just wanted to make sure you knew everything that I'd be getting into."

"So that's why you wanted to eat here rather than touring the campus?" I start to nod, then shrug. "It gives her something to do. I could potentially see the campus in the spring or summer, too. I know you have limited availability since the season is going on, so I appreciate you meeting with me at all."

"I can't ignore the top scorer in high school hockey asking to meet. I think I understand now why you aren't doing club." As I nod, Penny wiggles, looking toward the play place.

"If you don't mind, could we continue the conversation after we order? I told her she can't play until we get our food."

"You got it, and I'll pay for her too. After all, I'd pay for students and their parents - why not students and their kid?"

*****

Finishing eating, I let out a breath I didn't know I was holding. Penny has been playing pretty much the whole time, with only a few stops back to eat a chicken nugget here or a couple french fries there. My GPA is definitely high enough. The men's team has around a 3.5 usually and throughout high school I've been closer to a 3.75. I'm a good player, though it's a downside that I only played high school and not junior league. Coach is concerned about the fight, since he doesn't want me getting in any legal trouble once I'm on his team. Once I explained the circumstances, he was somewhat more understanding, though. He said he's not sure where we're at on scholarship availability, though. I should've signed years ago if I wanted a scholarship, but how was I to know what would be happening in our lives now.

"It was nice to meet you again, Hudson," he starts as he stands up.

"You too, Coach. I'll have to schedule a tour and maybe we can talk more then."

"Let me know, and, Hudson?" I look away from trying to find Penny in the maze of tunnels and look back to him. "I'm glad I got to meet Penny. She's sweet, and so well behaved. You've done well with her. You should be proud."

I smile. When so few people know, you don't get much encouragement. I definitely don't get much from my parents. All they tell me is what I'm doing wrong because she's going to behave like me rather than my perfect brother.

"Thank you, sir. I'm glad we could both come today." As I reach out to shake his hand again, he gives me another once over.

"One more thing."

Oh dear. "What's that?"

"I like my men to keep their hair above helmet line. I'm sure you're going for the hockey hair thing, especially if you might go to state, but you'd need a haircut to be on my team next year."

Running a hand back through my hair, I laugh. "You got it, Coach."

20

In English class on Monday, we get to do something different. Instead of the normal read an assigned section of chapters, interpret quotes and write who said them and all that stupid stuff, we're writing. There's a cart of chromebooks so we each grab one and we're told to open a google doc to work on our college application essays. We get three options of essay topics to pick from. We each get to pick partners to help us edit them and make them "the best that they can be."

Aliyah, sitting at the front of the room asks if she has to participate in this activity if she's already submitted her applications to colleges. Stupid overachiever girl. I know some colleges had those early applications due by now, but I was googling it the other night and a lot of places have them open until at least March, Though, I should decide in time for national signing day in a couple of weeks if I can. I do feel relieved when Mrs. Johnson tells her that she does need to do it because her essay can always be improved on and she could help others with theirs. She doesn't deserve to get out of an assignment just because she did her college applications early. Plus, then it'd be evident who hasn't submitted applications yet.

The three options for our topic are: "How will a particular major or program help you achieve your academic or professional goals?", "What you did to overcome a particular anxiety or phobia you had", and "A project or volunteer effort you led to help or improve your community."

After she puts these options on the projector at the front of the classroom, at least four hands go up around the classroom. How long does it need to be? At least 500 words. Can it be longer? Yes, but no longer than a thousand for the purpose of this assignment and it may depend on the school. Do we have to share it with someone? Yes, we need to practice taking criticism of our writing and we may be able to improve the content based on the suggestions we get.

I have a different question, though. "Do we need to pick one of those topics? I had been looking up some examples online the other day and I had a different one in mind." We learn that no, we don't have to pick from these options. She gives us the link for a website that has many examples for topics to make you think and that you want it to make sense for you. She just wanted to have some good, quick examples.

Piper looks like she's super in her head, not even realizing people were pairing off around her for the assignment, so I tap her on the shoulder. She jumps before turning around to look at me. "Hi there," I say, smiling at her.

"Umm, hi?" she half asks before looking around the room and seeing that pretty much everyone is working on their computers now.

"You willing to be my partner?"

"I figured you'd want Leo..."

"I already told him no. He's paired with Ash now," I roll my eyes. Leo is probably more than happy with working with Ashley. Before Piper can even look over at him, he throws a ball made of paper at my head. I'm not sure if this is toward my eye roll or just the fact that we're talking in general. Trying to hide her laugh, Piper nods her agreement to work with me before turning around to pull up the internet on her laptop.

As I watch her scroll through topic options, I pull up the essay on my google drive that I had started the other night and share it with her. Being grounded, I haven't had much else to do, so I've taken advantage of it to start looking into college stuff and seeing if I can figure out what I'm going to do with my life in four to seven months. Looking behind me and over toward Leo, I strategically angle my screen so it's almost facing the wall more than it's facing me. I don't want anyone reading this over my shoulder.

As soon as I see the notification of having shared the doc with her pop up on her computer, I start typing. Glancing back up, she reached the bottom of the list of topics. Instead of opening a doc to work, she turns to try to peek at my screen, but I fix my screen again to prevent her from messing up my strategy. Instead, she turns back around and opens my doc. As it's loading, I open a chat bar in my doc. "Watch the size of the doc and angle of your computer. I don't want people reading this."

"How small is your screen?"

"I have the doc at 70% and somewhat facing the wall. Should be small enough." Reading my doc, I can tell she decreases the size and adjusts her chromebook before moving her head closer to start reading it.

"You could do your own essay instead of reading mine."

"No thanks." She types back quickly. Too quickly. Something's up with her. I know she's never really brought up college, but is that the whole reason she's being weird?

Less than a minute after she started reading, I see her cursor show up at the bottom of the first paragraph before she turns around to look at me. I simply nod, and trace my eyes to the beginning of the essay to reread it. "I was forced to transfer schools at the beginning of my sophomore year after taking a year off school. Just about my entire freshman year, I was bullied because I had gotten a girl pregnant at the end of the summer before. Obviously, she was bullied too, but after she had the baby, she gave her up to me, and she didn't come back to school. I brought my newborn baby with me to school for the last 3 days of class until it was officially summer since I didn't have anyone to take care of her. I didn't expect her mom to give her up."

When a comment pops up, I click to check it out. She highlighted the part about bringing Penny to school and wrote, "Nothing like a hook." A few other comments pop up, but I don't open them. Instead, I look at the new message from Piper that popped up.

"You know you're going to have to turn this in to Mrs. Johnson, so she knows that you did the assignment, right? Someone besides me is going to know..."

"This is the best topic I have for a personal essay and you're the one I trust most to read and edit it for me. She'd be the teacher I most trust to know first." As she reads my response, the back of her neck turns red. Does that mean she's flattered?

*****

At lunch, we both order a la carte so we can bring our food wherever we please without having to worry about what to do with the trays. Since the blowup between me and Ashley, we haven't quite figured out where to eat. There aren't many open spots at tables that aren't basically claimed already. The theater kids sit on the stage that's in the cafeteria. The art kids usually go to the art room. The nerds go to the library for knowledge bowl. All the preppy kids are right by the condiments in the most convenient spot. It's not warm enough to eat outside. Today, we settle in a corner on the ramp between the office and the rest of the school. I only got fries with a side of cheese today, but I'm feeling a bit nauseous. Piper got chicken strips with a side of cheese and a chocolate milk.

"What's going on? You're barely eating when you usually get twice as much as me. Now you're not even talking."

I can't not tell her why I feel like this, "I told Mrs. Johnson that after I ate, I wanted to talk to her during lunch. Will you come with? I want to warn her before we have to turn in those essays." Just saying it out loud makes me more nauseated, so I push my fries away from me.

"Maybe talking before you eat is better so you can eat after you feel a little better?" Piper suggests.

I start to shake my head, but pause. "Do you actually think I'll feel better?"

"You'll either throw up and feel better, or you'll just feel better from talking. But either way, yes. For the record, I'd prefer you not throw up or I'm not kissing you the rest of the day and I'd really like to be able to kiss you still today."

"I suppose that's fair," I hesitate to agree, and still don't get up.

"It is, you're right. Now we're going to go talk. I'll carry the food in case you want to eat after." Piper stands, waiting in front of me to pull me to my feet before picking up the food in its paper trays off the floor. We walk down the ramp, and swing a right toward the high school hallway. Really, the middle school hallway houses the science one each of social studies and English, and a couple of math classrooms. The high school hallway has the rest of the social studies, Mrs. Johnson's room and most of the various extracurricular kind of classes like band, the computer lab, the library, and industrial arts. The art classroom is near the cafeteria and main office, separated from everything else. The halls used to be mostly separated by where the grades had classes, but the school decided it made more sense to house specialties together instead. The biggest thing with that, is they haven't moved the classrooms of existing teachers. Those are just moving as teachers retire out. Overall, the hallways are still labeled middle school and high school based on who has their lockers there – spending the most time there in the end.

Mrs. Johnson's door is closed when we arrive. Rather than going up to the door, I turn around about three feet from her door, mumbling something to Piper about our teacher being busy. Piper hooks her foot in front of my legs to stop me, having to hop a little to keep her balance as I walk into them.

"Knock," she orders firmly. I pause, debating my options. Rather than arguing, though, I turn around to do as ordered. I did tell her we'd be coming and I can't go against what I said. It's only a minute before the red-headed teacher opens the door.

"I didn't expect you until closer to the end of lunch!" she exclaims, looking at me. When she sees Piper standing behind me, she looks surprised. She drops her voice, but not so much that Piper isn't able to hear her, "I thought you said you wanted to meet with me privately?"

"I do, but Piper already knows what I want to talk to you about. She's holding me accountable that I do it. I hope it's okay we came earlier – I couldn't eat thinking about it. We could come back." I start to back away, but stop when I feel Piper's leg behind me, stopping me again.

"Of course, you should come in now." We both sit in desks in the front row of the classroom. As she grabs her rolling chair from behind the desk and centers it in front of us, she sits and asks, "Does it have to do with the assignment this morning? I noticed you two were acting strange and this one-" she nods at Piper, "-wasn't doing a whole lot of writing."

Piper speaks up, "For the record, it's because the topic I decided on was very personal and I didn't want to get emotional during class. I plan on working on it after school since I don't work today." She pauses, but when Mrs. Johnson doesn't answer right away, she adds, "Plus, he had written a lot before class and was my partner so I could read his and do my commenting and editing part."

"Okay, I don't expect you to hold back on the emotions if you're writing it at home, though. I want to feel what you're feeling." Piper doesn't look happy about this, but I figure it's the best opportunity for me to speak up.

"Anyways, the reason I wanted to meet with you-" I look to the door to ensure that it's closed before continuing, "is the topic of my essay. It's a topic that no teachers know about, and I don't currently have plans on anyone knowing. Piper is the only student who knows. My hockey coach knows, but he only found out when I recently got hurt." I pause, taking a deep breath. Am I ready to tell another person?

"The topic of my essay is my daughter." It's a simple sentence, but not so simple coming out of my mouth. When I look between the two girls, they're both waiting for me to say more. Our teacher is looking between Piper and I like Piper has the answers. I guess she probably has a lot of them, but not in the way she might be wondering. I'm just impressed she doesn't look completely shocked.

"Your daughter?" she finally manages to ask. I nod, just letting her take in the information. "How old is she?"

"She's three, almost four years old. She's the reason I transferred to this school."

"And I suppose she's also the reason some days you look like you're exhausted and almost dead to the world in my homeroom?" Mrs. Johnson tries to give me a stern look, but the friendly smile she pairs with it makes me laugh. She's not mad about it. She understands. She's a parent too.

"Generally, her paired with hockey, yes. I'm guessing you're referencing just before Christmas when I was up with her for a few nights. She had croup so we were rotating Tylenol and Ibuprofen to keep her fever down and had a humidifier going. It wasn't easy to sleep between doses of medicine with her coughing and trying to make sure she stayed elevated on the pillows."

"All that, and you still came to school and went to hockey without telling anyone what was going on?" When I nod, her eyebrows shoot up. "I probably would've given you a pass on some of that homework and napping if I had known."

"Exactly. I don't want a pass. I want to do it like everyone else. That's why I thought this would be a good essay topic. I'm in the top third of the class for GPA with my 3.5 and I've done it without any free passes because my teachers know how hard my life is. No one is taking it easy on me."

"So, you want to continue this secrecy?" With this question, I feel my jaw tighten as my stomach rolls again. I nod vigorously before she asks, "Is there anyone else who can know at this time?"

I hesitate before answering. I can tell she wishes she could tell even one person. Maybe the school social worker. I'm still not totally sure how we kept her from knowing. Nonetheless, I shake my head. "I've told so many people so quickly. I don't want things to change with my teachers right now. Plus, the more people that know, the higher the risk that someone lets something slip to a wrong person. I'm already a little uneasy about my hockey coach knowing, just because of his kid, Leo, being my friend. It'd be a little too easy to mention something wrong about me and my family and suddenly both his kids know. Please?"

Mrs. Johnson nods her head and smiles, making me sigh in relief. "Thank you for trusting me in telling me this information, Mr. Melville. May I ask her name?" When I tell her, she nods and says, "I do remember you mentioning a Penny in a journal. I just didn't know her relation to you." Before we leave the room, I give the teacher a hug as I thank her for listening and take my fries from Piper. Now I can eat.

*****

My game that evening is a double header. It's my first game playing again in over two weeks. Technically, I probably shouldn't be coming back yet, but it's nearly the end of the season and I'm going to need these last few weeks of games to make enough of a mark for any schools to still care about me. I've said no or pushed off too many schools for years and most of them probably don't even have any scholarship money left.

The girls are playing the first game, so the guys and I are in the bottom of the student section, watching. Piper and Penny are in their usual spots, front and center above the boxes. Knowing it was a double header, Piper brought a book she was excited to have bought called Tweet Cute. To keep Penny occupied while Piper reads, I put several books in her backpack to look at. At the end of the period, we'll go start getting dressed, but we were told we have to watch the girls' game until then.

When I feel a vibration on my wrist, I check my watch to see a text from Piper. "P at 4 o'clock." Crap. Piper has been trying to keep her amused the whole game. I'm honestly surprised it lasted this long, but why would she be amused by a hockey game I'm not playing in? She's not old enough to actually care about a game where she doesn't know anyone.

Standing up, I pull the attention my teammates have trained on the game to myself. Just what I need, them paying attention. When I turn around, Penny is practically right behind me. I try to smile like she's just a cute little girl I found behind me. I hope she doesn't realize what I'm doing.

"I bored. When you play?" she asks me. She could've called me Dad at the end of that sentence. It could be worse.

"We play in about 45 minutes. The girls need to finish and we need to get ready. Then we warm up and they zamboni before our game.

"But I bored! Why we here already?" She's using her hands to emphasize her point. I'm trying to shake my head at her, but it's too subtle. She isn't catching on. "Come sit with us!" Penny then says, pointing toward Piper. Great. Make it obvious that she truly knows me, versus me being the player who turned around at the wrong time.

"I need to stay here. I go get ready soon," I explain as gently as I can. I step up to the same level as her and she holds out her hand to take mine. I can't do that. Instead, I put my hand against her back to urge her to walk forward. My jaw hurts from clenching it. I'm trying not to be mad since she doesn't understand, but this could ruin it all with only a couple months left of school.

I lead Penny all the way back to Piper where she stands in front of her spot, waiting for me. Stopping a couple levels below them, I put my leg up onto the bench in front of me as I lean forward to be at a more even level with Penny's face. "I can't stay here. Did you need anything else?"

"I bored. Dinner?" Penny bounces on the balls of her feet, not catching on that I'm mad.

"Piper will get you dinner at the concession stand. There's money in your backpack like usual."

"I bored. When you play?" She already asked me this. Looking down to where my teammates are. Almost all of them watching us instead of the game now. The buzzer for the end of the period goes off.

"That noise means I should go start getting dressed. Anything else?"

"We ice skate after?"

"Not tonight. It'll be too late. Maybe another day. If you ask nicely and are good, maybe Piper will come with, too." When I glance back down to where we had been sitting, I find that the guys all went to the locker room. "I need to go get ready now, though. Be good."

Before Penny can ask any more questions, I take off down the benches to head through the tunnel to the locker rooms.

21

We end up losing our game. I didn't score at all. I just couldn't get into the zone after the thing with Penny. Some of them were look at me weird while we were getting ready. I'm just glad Penny fell asleep before she realized I wasn't going to score for her at all. When I finish changing, I head out to the benches per my usual routine. They're not there. Pulling out my phone from the back pocket of my dress pants, I text Piper. "Where are you?" I wait a minute, but no answer. I can only assume they went outside.

I look around outside the door, but don't find them there. When I bring my bag to my truck, they're not there either. Finally, I decide I need to find Piper's car. There aren't many cars left, and I know I need to find a blue Subaru. Looking around, there's only vehicle left in the lot that even looks like a Subaru, plus the snow that fell during the game is all melted off so it's likely been running a while. Luckily, it's only a couple of rows from mine.

Glancing into the back seat as I walk up, I see a sleeping child laid across the seat sideways. That's my little girl. I feel horrible about earlier, but I didn't have many options. It's not like when she came up to talk to me I could say, "By the way, guys, this is my daughter I've never mentioned. Isn't she cute?"

When I tug on the door handle, I just barely hear "-Hudson's life". Then silence with the realization that I'm there.

"What was that?"

"What was what?" Piper asks, looking over at me as I sit in the passenger seat. She's just sitting in her seat with her seatbelt unbuckled.

"You said my name." Her phone is in the cup holder and her car is way too old to voice text so that's not what she was doing. Penny is sleeping.

"It's nothing. It's stupid."

"You said my name, though. Please tell me."

"Okay," she hesitates, taking a deep breath. "I do this stupid thing where I ask my radio or iPod or whatever I'm listening to to tell me something. Usually it's how the day will go. Someone's impression of me. I'll specify the title or the song as a whole. Then, whatever the next song is that comes on, gives me insight. I asked for a song that describes your life." As she finishes, she nods toward the radio.

"That's not stupid." Taking a deep breath, I turn up the volume a little. Enough to hear, but not enough that the early aughts music will wake up Penny. "Dirty Little Secret," I say, letting out the breath. It doesn't take a genius to figure that out.

"You didn't text me back."

"I didn't see your text." She answers too fast. She saw it and just didn't answer. "Did they all figure it out?"

"I don't think so, but I don't think they're far off."

"You were so cold to her tonight. It was painful to watch."

"I have to be that way when there's people watching."

Before she answers, she reaches over to hold my hand, resting both of our hands in my lap. "You looked so mad, it was a little scary. Plus, you don't HAVE to be that way. People could know. You're almost done with school. It wouldn't matter anymore."

Pulling my hand out of hers, I say, "It would matter, though." She doesn't understand.

"Why?"

"It-" I run my hands through my long hair. How do I explain it? She just wouldn't understand. She's not keeping a secret from everyone at school. I just want to hit something with frustration. I set my fists on the dash in front of me, tempted to just let out a little annoyance. Instead, I cover my face. When I do, it seems like all of a sudden the volume goes up to at least 30. It's all I can hear. It's screaming at me. "It just would. Now could you please turn off that damn music?"

"Daddy?"

Crap. How loud did I say that? When I look in the back, I see Penny propped up on an elbow, rubbing an eye. I slouch back in my seat and wipe a hand down my face. "It's okay, monkey, we're going home soon. Piper, can you drive us around to my truck so I don't have to carry her all the way there?"

Piper hesitates like she's tempted to tell me to carry Penny after I just yelled. Instead, she shifts into reverse. When she pulls up next to the truck, I jump out before she's even shifted into park. Penny must be tired, because she's already half asleep again. Tucking my hands under her armpits, I lift her up, letting out a small grunt as my ribs decide that today has been too much for them. When I bring Penny to me, her head drops back, causing her to wake up and jerk her head forward. She just about gets my chin with her forehead which wouldn't have felt good for either of us.

"Easy there. We'll get you in your car seat and go home to go to sleep," I say, petting the back of her head until she leans it on my shoulder. She wraps her arms around my neck as I move to the passenger seat to put her in her seat.

"You mad no more?" she asks, playing with my hair as I try to set her down in her car seat.

"I wasn't mad, I was just…" I pause as I debate how to explain. I hate that she thought I was mad at her. When I finish buckling her up, I glance over my shoulder, Piper is standing there with Penny's backpack. "I was busy with my friends and needed to go get ready. I'm sorry." Turning around, I take the backpack from Piper and drop it on the floor in front of Penny's seat.

I close the door and catch Piper's hand as she's turning to get in her car. "I know you need to work on that essay tonight so that isn't really an option, but what do you work this week?" I want to redo tonight.

"Pretty much every day. Today and Saturday evening are my only open days. I work mornings on Saturday so I'm done at 2."

"Saturday afternoon, then. I work until 4, but we can get dinner and go to the mall or something?" I look at her pleadingly, hoping she'll fall for the puppy dog eyes. Penny had to have gotten that look from someone.

"Saturday afternoon. Meet you at the park and ride and then we can go to Kwik Trip down the road before we head up?"

"Deal. Now, are you too mad at me to kiss me?" I stick out my bottom lip for emphasis.

Finally, Piper smiles. Using the hand I'm still holding, she simply tugs on it to pull me closer. My free hand goes to the small of her back as I pull her all the way to me. With her free hand, she pushes it through my hair, still wet from the shower, and leaves it on the back of my neck. Deepening the kiss, I move my hand from the small of her back up her side. I barely get a feel of her breast before a horn honks next to us. Within seconds, we're each leaning against our own cars with my hands oh-so-casually covering the bulge in my pants. There may have been a lot of layers between us, but it was more than enough to turn me on.

"Get a room, you two!" Leo yells out the window that he rolled down. He and his brother Bryant are both in the car that Leo is driving.

"Fuck you, man," I answer, making Leo laugh before he drives away. I try to clear my throat, realizing my voice doesn't sound right. When I look back to Piper, she's looking toward my hands, noticing what they must be covering. I shrug, "I can't really help it." Moving towards her, I move close and ask, "Have I told you how gorgeous you are?" My voice still sounds off, but I'm just hoping that it sounds sexy rather than like a prepubescenct boy who's voice can't pick one octave.

It's amazing how fast her face can turn red as she smiles shyly. "Ummm, not in a little while. I don't know that I am, though."

My lips are only an inch from hers when I tell her, "Well, you're beautiful and gorgeous and I really, really like you a lot. I also really, really wish we weren't in a parking lot where people could see us so maybe I could make you realize that you are." I barely finish talking before she's kissing me again, that bulge pushing against her.

When she pushes on my chest, I take a step back. "I think you need to get someone home. I need to write an essay for you to edit." That was sudden. Were we going too fast? I take another step back before she adds, "I'll see you tomorrow at school." Before she slips back into her car, she gives me a quick peck. She isn't mad at least, but that doesn't really tell me if that was moving too fast.

I start my car quick so it can start warming up while I wipe all the snow off. On my last swipe of the snow, I decide to try Piper's game with the radio. When I turn on the radio, the song will tell me what Piper's thinking about us. I take a breath, hoping it's something good. I don't even realize I open the door, but I'm stepping in. I always turn off the radio before I turn off my car, so I have to turn it back on and turn the volume up before I know what it is. Lover by Taylor Swift. I don't really know this one, so I close my eyes and lean my head against the headrest while I listen to the whole thing. This has to be good. I think.

*****

22

Penny is brushing her teeth and I'm putting on flannel sweatpants to go to sleep. My phone pings with a text. I practically run across the room to where it's sitting on my bed, hoping it's Piper. I quite enjoyed the parking lot. I think she did too. I'm just hoping she won't get scared off like she nearly has before when we went too fast.

I sigh and nearly don't open it when I see the text isn't from Piper. It's from Bryant. "Dude. WTF?" Is he talking about Piper and me in the parking lot? It's not the first time. So instead, I just send him back a question mark.

Penny is done brushing her teeth, so I tuck my phone into my pocket and go into her room across the hall to check on her. Somehow, in the last minute or so, every pair of pajamas has been removed from her drawer so she can find the right ones. Of course, who knows if those ones are even clean. Instead, she settles for a different pair, and leaves me to refold all of them again.

Halfway through folding, my phone buzzes with a text, "The kid" is all it says. Okay, maybe they don't have it figured out. I set my phone next to me while I keep folding. What's my excuse?

Just as I fold the last nightgown, I look down to see another text came in. "Your kid."

"Fuck," I say out loud. "Shit," I add, looking over at Penny, looking at me with wide eyes. I don't swear around her. "Mmmmmmm I can't think of a better word right now that you're allowed to hear. Don't repeat those words."

"Those bad words, Daddy," she tells me, shaking her head emphatically.

"I know, I'm sorry, Monkey. Pick out a book so we can get you to bed." I can guarantee I won't be falling asleep reading with her tonight. I put the pajamas in her drawer and close it as she pulls a book off her shelf. Just as I'm ready to pick her up and drop her in bed, I hesitate. Maybe I shouldn't do unnecessary movements like that quite yet. It's a bit up in the air if I should be playing hockey again yet, but I pushed for that one.

Penny climbs up into the bed when I hesitate, scooting over toward the wall so I can climb in next to her. I grab my phone and pause, how am I going to explain this?

"Daddy," she whines. "Read."

Tucking my phone back in my pocket, I climb into bed beside her. Knowing I'll be sneaking away to try to call Bryant, I make sure she uses her pillow instead of my shoulder. Finally, she hands me the book. The Berenstain Bears and the Truth. It looks like it was a library book she picked this week. Well then. Nothing like a hint from the universe.

After the book is done, I give her a kiss and sneak out of bed, leaving her to fall asleep on her own. After all, she can't learn to fall asleep on her own when I'm in her bed every night. The book goes back on her shelf, I make sure her princess night light is on, and I close the door softly behind me. Pausing outside the door, I listen carefully and find the sound of pages turning. My mother is reading her book in the living room before bed.

I go into my room, toss a sweatshirt over my head and slip my feet into my slippers. It's cold outside.

"May I go outside to get some fresh air?" I'd rather ask for something simple right now than get in trouble for something stupid. My mother looks at me like I'm crazy, though.

"How far are you going that you're asking?"

"Just out on the deck or in the yard. Not far. Just wanted to make sure you knew where I was. Penny is in bed and I read her a book." My mother nods curtly, attention already back on the book. At least I know she apparently isn't paying attention to me. I open the sliding glass door next to the formal dining table and slip out onto the porch, closing it behind me. I still haven't answered Bryant. His last text was half an hour ago and now it's almost ten. Hopefully he's still up.

I click on the little phone icon as I shuffle down the steps to the deck that's nearly even height with the driveway. For once, I'm glad we shovel all of this. On the first ring, I debate hanging up, on the second ring, I question if he'll pick up after I didn't answer for so long. Finally, on the third, he does.

"Since when does a phone ringing take so long?" I try to joke, my voice sounding off. He doesn't say anything. The other side of the line is silent. "Ummm, are you there?" I ask, stepping down onto the driveway and wandering back toward the garage. Farther away from any windows near my parents is better.

"I'm here."

"So..."

"So, we know." I stop, taking a deep breath and putting my head against the door of the garage. How hard would I have to hit my head against this door to not remember anything? Probably not that hard with my recent concussion.

"How?"

"I mean, her talking to you today?"

"But-" I start, as if I can explain her away.

"She always comes to give you a high five after you score. You bring her home after every game. The car seat in your truck. The fact that you're never around on weekends. Our dad told us."

I pull my head away and punch the cold, metal door. It gives a little under my hand, but it hurts too. "Damn it."

"Did you really think no one was going to figure it out?"

I shake my hand in the air, seeing some spots of red coming to the surface of my knuckles. Just what I need, more injuries. "I hoped after my last school? People suck, man. They don't know when to stop. Especially when someone younger than you gets a girl pregnant."

"Wow..." I can't decide if he sounds pissed at me or at those people.

Probably me.

"I probably would've told you eventually. I just didn't know how. Especially after keeping it a secret so long. Did you really notice all those things?"

"I did. Leo didn't. He mostly only noticed her today. That was hard to miss. After I mentioned the other stuff at home, our dad told us."

"He wasn't supposed to tell you."

"It's better than Leo making guesses to every other idiot on the team and rumors spreading." I hit my forehead on the garage door. Just hard enough to feel it, but not hard enough to hurt myself. I almost expect him to say something about the sound of me hitting my head. It has to be loud enough to hear.

When he doesn't say anything, I ask, "Are you going to tell?"

"I won't. You need to talk to Leo, though. He's pissed. See you tomorrow." The call ends before I can say anything else.

I immediately try to call Leo. It barely rings before I'm sent to voicemail. End call. Call again. Voicemail. End call. Call again. Voicemail. He's pissed. Bryant is right.

"Leo. Please talk to me. I need to explain to you. Also, please don't tell anyone before I can talk to you. You need to know the whole story." I end the call. I stick my hand in a snow bank near my foot for a second of cold relief before I head back inside. It's going to be a long night if he doesn't call.

In my room, I see the book I borrowed from Piper sitting on the bed. I guess I'll read while I wait for Leo to call me back.

23

I stayed up way too late reading that book last night and hoping Leo would call. By the time I finished the book, I accepted he wasn't going to. I'm dreading getting to school. To put it off, I even tried braiding Penny's hair. It didn't go great. She wanted Piper to come do it instead.

At school, Leo isn't at his locker. When I walk past Bryant in the hallway, he avoids my gaze. As much as he sounded annoyed last night, I didn't think he'd ignore me. When I get to homeroom, Leo avoids talking to me or even looking at me too. This is the perfect example of why I didn't tell anyone. Two people know and now neither of them are talking to me. They don't want to be associated with someone who was too much of an idiot to use a condom. Why would they?

When Piper arrives, I can't bring myself to talk. Not when I give her the book back, not when she tries to make conversation. The most I say is asking her to help me braid and answering attendance.

When it comes time for English, we start talking about the essays. I read Piper's essay after she sent it to me. I tossed and turned when I tried sleeping, so I pulled it up on my phone. Raising my hand, I ask how to be an editor to a paper that has no grammatical errors.

We're instructed to make sure the essay has a good beginning, middle, and end. It needs to be detailed throughout, but also make sense. You shouldn't throw every detail in there just for fun. Make sure the end shows us a theme or something you learned from what you're writing about. Every section should say something rather than being overly wordy and it shouldn't be vague. Make sure nothing sounds awkward and everything should be realistic, not like you exaggerated it for the purpose of the essay.

That gives me a little bit to work off. She wrote it more like a story of what happened rather than an essay. When we grab the Chromebooks to get to work, there's a chat in the corner of Piper's essay as soon as I can get it open. "I just needed to get the words down when I was alone. Now I can edit it into an essay."

"Yup, I'm still making comments so I don't get docked for not doing it once it's perfect tho," I type back.

Piper isn't working on it as I'm making comments. When I look to her screen to figure out what she's doing, she has my essay open. Her laptop is strategically angled like it was yesterday, but I can tell what she's reading. I only added one sentence last night, several lines after the last in my essay. "I hate that I'm not her dad when I'm with my friends."

*****

Thursday night is the next game after Monday. Penny stayed at home with my mother. Piper is working. My father wasn't working the penalty box today. No one was there for me. My team wasn't even there for me. Leo is still ignoring me. Because Leo is ignoring me, so is most of the rest of the team. After all, Leo is coach's son. I can't score if I never get the puck. I was practically benched the last period because coach realized there wasn't a point in putting me in if I couldn't do anything. We lost 4-0.

By the time I got home, Penny was already in bed and asleep. I couldn't stop moving, pacing. Eventually, my parents told me I should leave or I'd wake her up. A week and a half ago I wasn't allowed to leave, now I'm basically being kicked out, at least, until I calm down enough to stop pacing.

Now, I'm sitting outside my truck, well, technically I'm more outside Piper's car. My truck is on the other side of her car I'm leaning against her driver's side door. She can't miss me that way. I have my feet planted on the ground with my knees bent in front of me. Too much. I'm a little bit dizzy and my life sucks. I lean my head against my knees and wrap my arms around my legs. I know she was working the later shift, but how late is that?

When I hear a voice say my name, I don't even pick up my head. That makes it worse. "Why'd you work so late?" I hear my voice ask.

She kneels in front of me when she answers. She must walk fast to already be to me. "You knew I was scheduled to work later than usual tonight. What are you doing here?"

"The game sucked. Leo hates me. You and my monkey are the only ones I have left." I feel like I'm going to start crying, just saying it.

"Where is she?" I finally pick up my head and find her looking around. Does she really think I'm stupid enough to bring her with me?

"Home. Sleeping. My parents said I needed to leave because I couldn't stop pacing and I'd wake her up. They just didn't know I stopped in the garage on my way out." As I finish speaking, I hold up the blue can next to me. I've been working on this one a lot longer than the others, partially because I didn't want to have to get up again to get another.

"How many have you had?"

"Maybe three or four?" I didn't count.

"Did you drive here like this?" she whispers.

"No!" I say this too loud. Or does it just seem louder to me? "I was waiting for you."

"And what am I going to do with you now?" She doesn't want me either.

"I'm fine. I'll go home," I say. When I stand, I realize that the dizziness that happened when I turned my head is much worse. I put a hand to the top of her car to catch my balance. "Maybe not."

She opens the door to the backseat of her car. As I'm about to ask what she's doing, she hands me a plastic bag. "Put the can in here and any other cans. We'll put it in my trunk. You can't have empty cans in your truck or you'll be in big trouble if you EVER get pulled over."

I make my way over to my car. It takes way too long to walk not very far when I have to keep hold of a vehicle. As I drop cans in the bag, I count. Four from the floor on my passenger door. I started drinking sitting in my car, but eventually decided I wanted air. Probably better than drinking in my car. She's right, that would get me in trouble.

"-have you eaten today?" Wait, did she say anything else? She pops the trunk of her car without being next to it. I drop the bag of cans in there.

Wait. Focus. She asked me a question. "I had lunch with you."

"And dinner?" I don't think I ate before the game. When I don't answer, she orders, "Give me your wallet and get in my car."

"My wallet?"

"Yes. You need food to soak up alcohol and I'm not buying." She holds out her hand. Feisty. I like it. I haven't seen Piper like this before. Wait, I have. A few weeks ago when I got hurt. Finally, I pull my wallet out of my pocket and drop it into her hand before I head to her passenger seat. She somehow makes it to her seat before I do. "Do I need to buckle you like a small child?" she asks. When I look over, I realized she's already buckled too with the car running.

"I don't need a seatbelt," I answer, trying to come up with an excuse for why I haven't done it already. When she shifts into drive, I almost smile. I won. Within a few seconds, though, she slams on her brakes. When the momentum forces me forward until I barely catch myself from hitting my head on the dashboard, I try to glare at her but crack a smile. Fine. Seat belt on. Once it's buckled, the car starts moving again. She doesn't even ask where I want to go. There's only so many options at this time of night, so we find ourselves at McDonald's within a few minutes. I order a Big Mac without onions, a large fry, and a coffee. I probably don't need caffeine, but coffee is what people always drink in the movies when they're hung over. Piper orders an Oreo McFlurry in addition to my food and I almost cheer when they don't say the ice cream machine is broken. It's a miracle!

It's only a few minutes before we have the food and my burger is beautiful. The first bite might be the best thing I've ever tasted. At least, until I put a fry in my life. My food practically disappears and I'm left watching Piper eat her ice cream. "So, what are we doing?" she asks.

The food must be sobering up because I have a realization. "I really don't think I can go back to my parent's house." I put my head in my hands. The world isn't spinning anymore, but I really don't want to get yelled at tonight.

"Are you even ungrounded yet? How are you going to justify not going home tonight?"

"I have my phone, so I'm mostly ungrounded. You're always a little grounded in a way when you have a kid to take care of since you have to be home." I nearly cringe when I say that out loud. It sounds so much worse coming out of my mouth than it did in my head.

"So, justification? You have to warn her this time. It's a school night."

Shit. It's a school night. I had barely picked my head up out of my hands, but I drop it back down. Into my hands, I suggest, "I could tell her the truth? I'm at my girlfriend's house because I'm drunk and can't get home?" Piper snorts. I'm not even sure which part of that statement the snort is to. I barely remember what I said other than suggesting to tell them I'm drunk. "You're right. I could say I didn't realize how late it got and I'm staying at Leo's house?"

"But would she call there to make sure it's true?" she asks.

"No, she's probably sleeping. Just to have some confirmation in a text that I'm not home. I bring Monkey to daycare tomorrow, though. Think we could go back to get the car seat out of my truck and do that tomorrow so I can shower and change before school?" Hesitantly, Piper nods her agreement.

*****

When we get to Piper's house, it's just how I remember it. This time, though, Piper leaves her shoes by the door and brings mine with us to the bedroom - once again hiding my presence. This time when we lay down, though, I can lay however I want. As much as I want to face her, I can't see her in the dark of the room anyways. She has blackout curtains so not even a street light illuminates the room. Instead, I lay how I'm comfortable. On my back with one arm behind my head. Usually, my other arm would be by my side, but instead, Piper is using it as a pillow with the rest of my arm wrapped around her.

We lay in comfortable silence for a couple of minutes before Piper asks, "Why do you think Leo hates you?"

"He knows." Somehow, I haven't told her all week, but sometimes it's easier to talk about things in the dark.

"He knows...?" she asks. She barely pauses, obviously registering it before she asks, "How?"

"Bryant told me. He saw the car seat that night in my truck. When they got home, they were talking together about everything with Penny. Bryant mentioned the car seat, so their dad told them."

"But, why would he be mad?"

"How the hell would I know? It isn't his life that seems to be splintering every time he turn around." Volume. Breathe.

"Maybe he's just mad that he didn't find out from you, his best friend. He had to find out from his dad." I swear I feel wetness on my arm like Piper is crying, but she doesn't betray anything by the sound of her voice or her breathing.

Could Leo's whole problem be that I'm not the one that told him? He is a good guy. "I suppose. I really hope he doesn't tell anyone else, though." Piper doesn't answer me. We're both silent for at least a full minute before I turn toward her, giving her a kiss. "You know you're the best thing that's happened to me since Penny, right?"

"I don't-" When it sounds like Piper's going to argue, I kiss her again. I want her to know how much I appreciate her. I put my free hand that isn't tucked under her behind her neck and pull her in deeper, wedging my body closer to her as well.

"You're beautiful. And you're so sexy, especially in this." I tug at the tiny strap of the tank top she's wearing. Her face is tucked against my shoulder, so I kiss her neck. Using my body to turn her onto her back, I start kissing downward and pause at the top edge of her tank top. "Is this okay?" She nods and I start kissing again, starting at her mouth again. This time, though, I don't stop where her clothes start.

I don't do much before she pulls my face back up to her mouth. While I kiss her, my hand travels south to fiddle with her shorts. She nods, so I finally free my second hand to pull at the sides of her shorts. When she lifts her bottom up, the shorts slide right off along with her underwear. Initially, she doesn't move much other than groaning and lifting her hips. Then, she reaches out her hand to touch the bulge in my sweatpants. When she does that, I have to pause what I'm doing. Why does this feel so good through two layers of clothes. When she moves her hand, I know I need more. I pull down my sweatpants, but not my boxers yet. I don't know if she's ready to go that far.

Moving my body between her legs, I go back to kissing her. Her lips, her neck, her chest. Everywhere. We're just about there, it's just the thin layer of boxers between. "More. Please," she gasps.

When I pull down my underwear in response, her eyes widen. "Are you sure?"

"Do you have a- a- you know?" I'm not sure if it's shyness, or a loss for words, but I can't help but smile a little bit. On the floor now, I look for my wallet in my pockets unsuccessfully. Finding it on the dresser, I open it to the cash pocket. "I haven't needed one in so long. Damnit." I set the wallet back down and run my hands through my hair. There's nothing there. Why am I such an idiot? Obviously I wasn't expecting this tonight, but I should've learned better years ago.

"Come here," Piper says, gently. When I trudge over to her, her arms are out, ready to hug me. When I sit on the edge of the bed, I just face away from her. "It's okay. We don't need to tonight. It was probably a little quick anyways."

I turn to face her. Is she just trying to make me feel better? "Are you sure? We could just, you know, do it?"

"I think that's probably what got you into the situation you're already in." Well, that thought is a boner killer.

"You're right," I answer, giving her a quick peck on the lips as my hands drift down. "Are you sure you don't want me to finish you?"

"I think I'll be okay." I sense, rather than feel or see her shrug.

"Well, I need to wash my hands," I answer after assessing her. She's really just fine? If I wait now, I'll have blue balls.

When I get back, Piper is already dressed again and looks ridiculously comfortable, sleeping on her stomach hugging her pillow. When I lay down, she turns on her side so that I'm spooning her. I tuck my arm around her to pull her nice and close and we sleep like that until my alarm goes off in the morning.

*****

Beep. Beep. Beep. "The time is 6:30am." My phone says before it starts beeping again. When I don't reach to turn it off immediately, Piper kicks my leg and pulls a pillow over her head. The noise and light hurts my eyes. Sleep will fix it. Instead of finding my phone, I put my arm around Piper to pull her closer again.

Rather than settling back in, Piper pushes my arm away. "Turn that stupid thing off. Please." Finally, I roll out of bed and find my phone, silencing it. "Much better," she sighs, pushing the pillow off her head and looking at me.

I blink quickly a few times before muttering, "It's too bright," and squeezing my eyes shut again.

"That would be called a hangover. You need water, ibuprofen, and to get up because you need to go home and get ready for school and bring You-Know-Who to daycare."

"Does Voldemort go to daycare?" I ask, unable to withhold the reference. I manage to sound so serious, that Piper starts giggling.

"I really hope you don't call her that," Piper answers, crawling out of bed to head out of the room. I get dressed while sh's out of the room and when she's not back right away, I start looking through her drawers. I'll pick out her outfit.

By the time she comes back, I have an entire outfit laid out on the bed next to me. The outfit constitutes yoga pants, a bra, a thong, and a light pink sweater. "Wow, you want me to go all out on a school day, except with yoga pants to throw the whole thing off. If I didn't know better, I'd think you just want to check out my butt." She turns around as she gets dressed, but I manage to catch a couple glances of her body.

"That may be a good part of my motivation for getting out of bed this morning," I answer, standing to get nice and close to me before kissing her. She only has the pants and bra on so far. She wiggles out of my arms to move to the closet.

When I start to argue that she's getting different clothes, she says, "Chill, I need a tank top or something to go under this sweater." I say.

As I watch her walk around her room, I realize I tried to leave a hickey on her neck last night and now I don't see it. "Shouldn't there be...?" I start before moving a wave of hair away from the left side of her neck. When I touch the spot where it was, I realize I can just barely see the color. "You're wearing makeup. Like full makeup, aren't you?"

"I might be," Piper smirks, pulling the sweater over her head on before putting her finger to her lips to signal me to stop talking. She picks up her phone, backpack, and clothes like she usually wears at work before she opens her door. She creeps out and comes back with her shoes on and purse and keys in hand before she signals for me to follow her.

On the way to my house, we stop at Kwik Trip to get me a coffee and ibuprofen. I tell Piper to find herself something and she comes back with a milk and a double chocolate chip muffin. We make a stop at Subway to get the car seat before our next stop. At the house, she parks on the road while I head inside. She's in charge of getting the car seat in while I get ready. Quick, cold shower, get dressed in jeans and a long-sleeved shirt, and collect Penny. My mom did get Penny ready this morning, which helped.

When I walk out of the house, Penny's hand in mine and my backpack over my shoulder, she automatically starts moving toward where my truck is usually parked. When she looks to me confused, I point to Piper's car. Recognizing it, Penny runs across the grass straight to the car.

"Wow, you're a new person," she jokes as I buckle Penny in and make sure the seat is tight enough.

"The shower helped," I answer, pushing my hair back out of my face before I shut the door.

When I open my door, Penny yells, "You stinky today, Daddy!"

Reaching back to tickle her, I ask. "Are you sure about that, you little gremlin?" She giggles and shouts for me to stop so I put on my seat belt. She ran into me before my shower and based on her reaction, I'm surprised Piper let me anywhere near her.

As Piper puts the car into drive, she adds, "You were a little bit stinky this morning. I hope you brushed your teeth too." With a grin, I lean over and breathe on her before I kiss her cheek. "Much better. Now where are we going?"

24

On Saturday, I get to the park and ride before Piper. I almost decided to bring Penny with, but even with some people knowing, I was still too anxious about bringing her out where anyone could run into us. Leo and Bryant are still ignoring me, but other people don't seem to know everything, just that those two are mad at me. Occasionally, my mom is in agreement to watch Penny, but not often. I think this time she only agreed because I've been taking care of her so much more after hurting myself. With how strung up I've been since the beginning of the week, even she thought I need a little break.

It isn't long that I'm sitting there before the passenger side door gets opened. I jump a little, before I look over and see Piper climbing in. I can see her car behind her, so she parked right next to me. Inside, she sets her purse on the floor and looks around. "This is the first time I've sat in your truck. It's really roomy."

Closing the app I was using to make an appointment, I set my phone in the cup holder and slide across the bench seat to give her a kiss. She gives me a kiss, but when I try to deepen it, she says, "Just drive." Per our previous agreement, we stop to get snacks at Kwik Trip before we get on I-35 to head to Duluth.

"Do you mind if I change up the plans just a little bit?" I ask, looking over. I know we had discussed already, but I want this to be a little more of a date.

"What did you have in mind?"

"Well, maybe bowling? We could have pizza while we bowl so we still get dinner in. Then we go to the mall after that?"

She looks like she thinks about it, but not long before she answers, "I think bowling sounds fun!"

"I do have one other stop before bowling, but it should be quick." When she looks like she's about to ask what it is, I add, "It's a surprise."

"So, how did it go with Leo?"

I can only grimace, but that makes her nervous based on the look on her face. "I mean, he talked to me. Basically, you were right. He was pissed that he didn't know something so important and he had to find out from his dad. Some of the team had guessed in the locker room and he defended me I guess."

"Well, that's nice," she attempts

"It's nice. It's also a big part of why he was so mad. He defended what was actually right and he always assumed the best of me."

She doesn't answer, but she must be thinking the same thing I am. He shouldn't have to defend me. I shouldn't have a secret like this. But also, I'm not sure I'm worth defending. Instead, after a couple of minutes, she changes the subject. "So, the other night…"

Reaching over, I take her hand and squeeze it. "Yeah?"

"You said you haven't, um-" When I look over to smile at her encouragingly, I find her face bright pink. I can barely keep myself from laughing.

"Does your face always turn this red when you talk about anything intimate?"

"I wouldn't know. So, you know. You said you haven't needed a condom in a long time. What does that mean?"

Oh. Serious conversation. Not joking conversation. "Well, Penny is almost four. So, it's been a little over four years since anything. Even if I still had one in my wallet, it would probably be expired by now." When she's silent again, I look over. Her mind is racing. I realize I've never really asked about her history. "How about you?"

"Never," she mumbles. Never never? Like, anything? I snap my head over to see if she's being serious, but she's already looking at me nervously. When she sees me looking at her, she slumps in her seat.

"So that's why you panicked at my parent's house?"

"Possibly?" She slouches a little further. If she goes much further, she's just going to be on the floor.

"And the other night?"

"That's not a full question," she deflects.

"Was that the first time you touched, or saw, anything on a guy?" That could explain her reaction.

"I saw your chest and abs when you broke your ribs," she points out halfheartedly. I squeeze her thigh a little. Not what I meant, and she knows I'm thinking it. "Yeah, it was."

When I turn over my hand resting on her leg, she takes it. "I wish I had known. I was still drunk. That wasn't my best. I could've done so much better for you."

Even without her answering me and with an eventual subject change, we arrive at our first stop. "A salon?"

I nod. "I'll be back in about 25 minutes." When I tell the stylist, she looks shocked but agrees. She starts with tying off my hair and putting it into braids. Once all the sections are braided, she grabs the scissors. When she places the scissors at the base of the braid, I close my eyes. I want to wait to see until she's done.

My head feels lighter. She's been cutting for what feels like forever, but it's only been a few minutes. I didn't realize how heavy my hair was. She runs her hands through my hair a couple times before saying, "You're all done." I finally open my eyes and it's a shock. My hair is down to a couple of inches. She put gel in it to tease the hair up off my forehead and to my right. The sides are shorter than the top. I think I like it, more than I liked it when it was short when I was younger. Maybe it's just that I'm older now and my face looks different.

"Close your eyes until I get out there," I text Piper as I get up to pay. I thank the stylist, and head outside. When I get to the car, Piper's eyes are closed per instructions. Her face is flat, so I don't think she's peaked. She'd probably be reacting somehow if she saw.

Once I'm in the car and close the door, she asks, "Can I open my eyes now?" When I agree, she opens her eyes and her mouth immediately drops open. Crap. Does she hate it? The longer she looks at me, her mouth hanging open turns into a smile. Good sign. "You know, when I asked what you look like with shorter hair, I didn't actually mean that you should cut it off."

That doesn't sound great, though. I move my hands as though I'm going to push my hair back, but I don't have all the hair to push back out of my face. "You don't like it?"

"No, I do." She moves closer to me on the bench seat to reach up and touch my hair. It's not hard and gross like hair can get with gel in it. It mostly just feels like my hair. "I really do." With that, she kisses me. One of those kisses with her hand on the back of my neck to pull me in and hold me close.

The bowling alley isn't far away, but practically the whole drive, she's looking at me like she's studying for a test. Once there, I get us a lane and we each get shoes.

We flirt as we bowl. She sucks at bowling. Half the time, she's lucky if she gets even 3 pins down. Because she's so bad at bowling, I give her a kiss each time she gets any down. She keeps looking at me, like she's admiring my new look. At one point, I even push her up against a column near our lane and made out with her. I love getting to spend time with her. Eventually, after a lot of convincing, she gets me to agree to take a selfie with her. My one condition, I'm also allowed to take a funny one. She isn't prepared, so when I stick out my tongue and do the peace sign, she starts laughing. A pizza – half pepperoni and half sausage and green pepper – is split between us.

After two games, we head to the mall. There, we park by the bookstore entrance. Inside the bookstore, we look at the kids books. When Piper spots Three Little Pigs, she convinces me we have to get it since she needs to understand what we were trying to get her to say. Along with the book for Penny, I convince Piper to pick out a book. "I always have a book in mind in case I decide to splurge and buy one," she says as she walks straight up to the back side of the Young Adult section where the beginning of the alphabet of contemporary is. There, she finds an author, and I watch as she scans through the titles, grabbing one. She turns around with a smile on her face, hugging the book to her chest. "The most recent Sarah Dessen book. I've collected most of her books from garage sales, but I haven't been able to find this one."

Next, we go to Old Navy. We do a quick lap of the store first and then go back to the little kid section. Penny is going to need 4T spring and summer clothes soon enough and would probably appreciate someone other than me picking them out. Piper laughs when I tell her that, but nonetheless looks through the clothes, finding a couple of pairs of shorts, something she called a skort, and some shirts. Almost every time I pick up an outfit and show it to Piper, she vetoes it while barely even looking up. The only suggestions she accepts from me are a couple dresses and a cute yellow rain jacket with blue rain drops on it. I try not to grimace at the amount that I pay before we leave the store. A lot of times, I buy her clothes at a second hand store, but a mall date seemed like a good excuse to buy something new.

Next up is the toy store. I nearly run into someone as I turn the corner. Abruptly stopping, I take a step back and look at the girl. She has brown hair and dark blue eyes. Penny's are lighter than hers, more like mine. Penny has her face shape, though. It's Maci. She's just like in my dream. She's skinny. Skinnier than she ever was in school.

"Oh, hi," I say, surprised.

I don't think she even recognized me at first. Not until I said something and I sounded like I knew her. Then, she looks up to my face and asks, "I thought you were going to grow your hair out?" like I've seen her any time in the last 4 years.

"I did grow my hair out. I just cut it." I don't know why I'm explaining myself to her.

"Well," she looks pointedly at Piper, "You shouldn't let a girl tell you what to do."

"I didn't. I'm doing it for my future."

"Your future? You probably don't have much of a future when you're probably here to buy a toy for your daughter."

"You mean, our daughter?" Maci looks shocked when I say that, then checks with the boy next to her. He's looking at her, looking to verify what I just said. He doesn't know. Why would he?

"I wouldn't know. For all I know, you have another one," she pauses and looks pointedly at Piper. "Or maybe one on the way. Might as well with no future ahead of you." Piper drops my hand, taking a small step back. She has stuck by me, but that's when pretty much no one knows. Maci knows more than Piper does.

"At least I've grown up. More than I can say for the girl who ditched her daughter for the last four years." Might be a low blow, but I felt the need to come back with something.

"It's not ditching when I didn't want her in the first place. If it wasn't for you and your family, she wouldn't have even been born. You were well aware I wasn't going to see her." With that, she walks away, holding the boy's hand and pulling him with her.

When they get far enough away, I turn to Piper. "Are you okay?" She nods, albeit, hesitantly. I take her head before asking, "Did you still want to go to Legacy?" With her agreement, we head in.

Right at the entrance of the store, there's a T-Rex that's bigger than me. We look at some of the cars, then stuffed animals. The books are one area where Piper gets distracted, insisting we need to get Penny a book even though we just got her one. Then, she finds a doll section. Not only are there dolls, but there are doll strollers, clothes, accessories, and cribs. She points at a little, cloth stroller that would be the perfect height for Penny to push her doll around when going for a walk that I immediately takes off the shelf. We glance at puzzles and board games for both adults and kids, but manage to walk away without buying anything from there. I pay for the stroller, and we head back into the main section of the mall, back towards where we came in.

When we make it back to the truck, I turn on the radio. Plugging my phone into the radio, I turn the radio on and the volume up. The song that comes on is Lose Yourself. With the face she makes to the rap, I hand my phone over for her to pick. She looks like she's thinking before she simply clicks next. I bet she's doing her radio game.

Second Chance.

"You're being so quiet," I point out, looking over to her and offering my hand.

She takes my hand. "My radio game." She shrugs, like It's not a big deal.

"So, what was that one?" I'm curious.

"What I should do now, after that run in."

"Well, I hope you listen. So what's the next question?"

"The next song title will tell me how you feel about me," she answers. She almost looks like she's hoping I'll verify or refute the result. "Sometimes I'll skip to the next one, sometimes I'll wait. What do you want me to do?"

"Skip. I'm curious."

I'll Be.

"So, since the title only half answers, then do you take context from the lyrics?" I know she explained this the other day, but she didn't explain this that much.

"Exactly. But if it was an answer in and of itself, we would leave it at that." She pauses while we wait and listen.

With the lyrics, I say the words "we belong together" making her smile in relief.

"Do you have any questions for the universe?"

After a long pause, he finally answers. "What do I do?" She looks at me expectantly. "Skip. I can't wait."

She does as I ask. Breaking the Habit. "Well, I guess that's self-explanatory," I say after a minute of listening to it. When she looks confused, I add, "Lying to everyone about her is my habit. I need to break it."

25

Finally, senior night is here. Practically the entire team has been icing me out for two weeks. Leo finally started talking to me again last week. It's a good thing, too. It required his dad being in on it to plan Senior Night like it needs to be. Like I need it to be. That sounds like it's my night. I know I'm one of five seniors, but it feels like my night. My parents are coming to my game tonight, Penny is sitting by them so Piper doesn't have to babysit her, and my secret will be out.

I'm sitting in my truck. It's 5:00. My head drops to the steering wheel. I need to go inside, but I don't know that I can. I'm early, but I planned to be one of the first ones there so that I'm ready before everyone else. I told Coach Scott I wanted to talk to the team before we went out. I take a deep breath, and open the car door before I can stop myself. It's getting cold in here anyways.

My breath shines in the cold air outside. I grab the strap of my hockey bag and pull it out of the back. I can do this.

Getting dressed in the locker room, Leo and Bryant are the next ones to get here. They give me a confused look when they see me already there and nearly dressed.

"I need to talk to everyone, players only, before we go out. I didn't want to do it while I was getting ready." They both nod their assent. Leo helped me figure this out with his dad. Bryant must just understand. Or Leo told him. "I'm going over to the barn for a few minutes. I need to skate. I can't just sit here and wait."

"Don't ruin your pretty hair before pictures with your family" Leo says as I head toward the door. When I turn around, he's smirking. "Or, I think I know someone else that would want a picture with you and that pretty head of hair." Piper has been all over me since I got my haircut, constantly running her hands through it and kissing me.

I flip him the bird as I walk away. The barn is the rink next door. We can walk between them with our skates on because there isn't a locker room over there and there's no one in there now. It tends to be colder. Almost cold enough to ice out your thoughts. Plus, I won't get in trouble for being on the fresh ice right before game time.

I skate a few laps as hard as I can before I slow down. Leo is right, my parents wouldn't be happy if in the pictures they got with me, I was all sweaty. As I skate, I go through the words I rehearsed over and over.

"Melville!" I stop skating when I hear my name. "If you don't come talk now, we're going to go out without you," Leo yells from the entrance.

I skate towards him, following him back to the locker room. "Everyone there?"

"You got it," he answers before he opens the door, striding in on his skates. I follow him in and stop just inside the door. When it slams behind me, everyone looks up.

"Umm, hey guys," I say, rubbing the back of my neck. I hear someone snort. For a captain, I'm super convincing these days. When I look around, almost no one is looking at me already.

"Look, I know you guys are probably pissed at me. Yes, I have a daughter. She's almost three years old. I didn't tell anyone because I was bullied enough at my last school that I left. I didn't want that to happen here."

"You think we're like that?" One of the guys yell.

"I didn't know what to expect when I started at a new school. The game I got in a fight at was my old school. You can see how much they loved me." That quieted them down. Now they all seem to be watching me. "The thing is, the last couple months, I've realized how crappy it is that I've kept her a secret. For me, for you, and most of all, for her. I don't want to do that anymore. I want people to know about her because she's so sweet and smart and she loves watching us play.

"I want all of you to know her."

It's silent. I look up at the clock. We need to get out there in a couple minutes. "What do you guys say? Do you forgive me for being an jerk?"

Everyone looks around at each other. Bryant and Leo both say in unison, "I do."

Brayden shrugs and says, "I suppose." After that, there's a general ascent from the rest of the team.

"Great, then let's go get senior night done, so we can play some hockey!" With that, cheers go up. We move out to our entrance to the rink.

I open the door and pause, waiting for the cue. While I wait, I look up at the stands. Piper and her friend Kaelyn are sitting in the normal spot. I don't see my parents or Penny. They must be at the door waiting with the parents. Are all the parents really confused by Penny? Are my parents explaining to everyone, or just letting them be confused? I step back, away from the ice. I feel like I might throw up.

I squat so my head is as close to between my knees as it can get with all the padding. When something hits me, I nearly tip over. It was a helmet, Leo's to be exact. "Dude. Stand up. You're going to be fine. She's the perfect size that I'm going to find an Otter costume for her when you get us to State. No one can dislike an otter and no one can dislike the father of a cute otter."

"Here's our Otters!" our announcer yells. Our cue. I wave for the team to go. Everyone skates a couple laps before going to line up. The seniors were told to drop helmets and sticks in the box. Everyone else could wear their helmets and keep their sticks. Leo and I follow last. Helmet and stick in the box, check. The non-seniors line up in two lines on the side of the Dragons so we have to skate between them to the middle of the rink. The seniors line up along the wall in the order we'll get called. I'm last. At least Leo is next to me.

First, Hunter is called and everyone claps. They say his position and his parents names. He skates between the lines of underclassmen hitting their sticks against the ice straight across where he gets the rose that he'll give his mom. As he skates kitty corner across the ice to the other blue line- crap, what if I totally biff it skating across the ice? - they say that he played hockey, football, and baseball in high school and plans to go to Michigan Tech for Biomedical Engineering and plans to play hockey there. Hunter gets across the ice and steps onto the carpet they set out for the parents to walk out on. There, he meets his parents, gives his mom the single rose, and gives her a hug. He gives his dad a hug as well and they pose for a picture. Everyone in the stands claps again.

This happens three more times until it's just Leo and me waiting. Before he gets called out, he taps me. When I look over, he symbolizes taking in a big deep breath, and letting it out. We both do it once, and he's called. Crap, I'm next. Leo does it a little different than the other four before him. He grabs our goalie's hockey stick at the end of the line of underclassmen, pulling Bryant with him before he goes to get the rose. First, he takes a picture with just his parents, then he makes Bryant take off his helmet to take a picture with them. I hear the crowd awwww.

Piper and Kaelyn are both looking at the two, smiling. Piper then starts whispering and nudging at Kaelyn. It's nice to see her interacting with someone our age besides me. Bryant comes back to the line up of underclassmen while Leo and his parents go to the group on the end of the rink where they're awaiting the group picture.

Finally, it's my turn. I skate across to get my rose and have two waiting for me. I'm not listening to what they say, just for when they say that I'm inviting my daughter Penny out for senior night since she's a big part of my family. I get to the end of the carpet before my family does.

When I stand there facing them, Penny starts running toward me. My mother is wearing my jersey since Penny would be practically drowning in it, but we found her a long sleeve that matched pretty closely and is her size. As she reaches me, she holds out her arms and jumps, forcing me to catch her and swing her up in the air. I give her a hug and pull away to hand her one of the roses. She wraps her arms around my neck as I step up to give my mother her rose and a one-armed hug, which is the best I can do while I'm holding Penny.

"I don't think you need to worry, this time," she whispers in my ear as I'm bent over to hug her. I'm nearly a foot taller than her when I'm on my skates. That's when I notice how loud the cheers are. They weren't this loud for everyone else, at least, I don't think so.

I release my mom and hug my father. He doesn't say anything, but there's a slight shine to his eyes. Is he crying? My mother moves to my right and my father to my left. I shift Penny so she's somewhat facing the camera and point her to where to look. On the count of three, we all say "Hockey!" The photographer also insists on a picture of just Penny and I as my parents move over to the rest of the group. Finally, a big group picture is taken with all the senior families and, before I can release Penny to go back to the stands with my parents, Leo comes up to us.

"Hi, Penny, I'm Leo." She hides her face in my jersey, so I spin around so Leo is behind us and looking at her again. "I'm your dad's best friend." With that, she looks up at me, quizzically. When I nod, she finally looks at him, not so scared anymore. "Do you want an otter costume so you can be our mascot for the rest of the year?"

"Can I?" she asks me, her eyes lighting up.

"His dad is the coach. I think if he's asking, you probably could. We might have to teach you how to skate, though," I answer, tickling her.

"Yes yes yes!" She throws her arms around my neck again and I skate towards where my parents are waiting at the doors to leave the rink.

"You go sit by your grandparents during the game. Be my good luck charm. I love you."

"Love you." I drop her to her feet on solid ground and she waves as she runs off, blowing me a kiss. I pick up my helmet and stick from the box and it's time to get warmed up for the game. Hopefully this goes better than other games have been going lately.

*****

After I get home from the game, I text Piper. "Watch the news at 10 on channel 6!" When I saw her after the game, I forgot to tell her about it. I already put Penny to bed, but my parents and George are still up. I can't believe George came home. He never comes home between holidays anymore. Obviously my parents knew what I was doing, but the fact that he came home for my senior night? He must've known too.

We gathered in the basement so we can all watch the interview. Mother and father are both sitting on the couch. George is lounged in the bean bag chair. That leaves either the couch between my parents or the papasan chair for me. Instead, I can't even sit down while I wait for the interview. I keep going upstairs to make sure Penny is still asleep. When I do manage to sit down, it's for a maximum for five minutes on the floor in the center of the room.

As I come back down from checking on Penny, about halfway through the news, I hear them say, "The boy who's been scoring most of the points for the Otters has not only been putting in a lot of work on the ice, but also at home."

It cuts to a clip of me in my interview, "Well, of course I have to work hard at practice. I also work on the weekends when I don't have practice and I take care of my daughter in the evenings. She goes to daycare when I'm at school." I shrug in the video. It cuts to a clip of Penny running out to me during senior night.

The voice-over starts talking again. "You heard that right. He has an almost four year-old daughter that he actually left school to care for for her first year."

"I almost didn't start playing hockey again. I wasn't sure I could handle everything and keeping my grades up. Leo talked me into it, though."

"Leo, a fellow senior who gave Hudson two assists on his three goals tonight. Hudson told us that he's been looking at different schools, but he hasn't decided for sure where he's going yet. He wasn't willing to tell us any of his thoughts in case something didn't pan out."

And just like that, it's over. As the news woman changes the topic, my father turns off the tv. George finally says, "You're going to college?"

"Dude."

"What?"

"Do you have to make it sound like it's impossible?"

"You have a kid. Do you really think you can go to college?"

"I'll have done three years of high school and hockey. Why can't I do college and hockey? College takes less time."

"You just don't get it."

"You just don't get that I want us to have a good life. I don't want to rely on mother and father because I did something irresponsible when I was young." My parents were silent throughout the entire conversation, and now, I'm over it. I'm going upstairs. I grab my phone from the floor and go up to my room. Peeking in Penny's room, I see that she still looks like she's sleeping so I sneak into my room and close the door. There, I click Piper's name and call her.

"I saw your interview," she says first thing when she answers.

"Yeah?"

"Yeah. You did great! You looked so casual and confident. How did you feel?"

"Not like that. By then, I mostly felt better, but during, I honestly felt a little nauseous."

"Am I allowed to know what colleges you're looking at?"

"Well, that's part of the problem. I thought I talked with UMD but I apparently didn't pay enough attention to the signature on the email or something. After the game I talked with the scout again and it was Minnesota. I can't go three hours away with Penny."

"I can send my tape to a couple of local schools. I have some ideas.

"Who?" She sounds so excited.

"UWS or UMD."

"Seriously?" She sounds incredulous.

"What's wrong with that?" I've never heard anything bad about them.

"Nothing. I'm waiting on an acceptance letter from UWS, too. I applied there."

"We could both go there?"

"We could, if we both get accepted." With that, all I hear for a second is a high-pitched, excited, I assume, squeal.

26

I spent most of the night Friday emailing coaches and sending them tapes. Saturday, I was able to meet with the UWS coach. They're only D2, but that means it isn't quite as competitive. It also means if someone decides not to play hockey there, I might be able to get a partial scholarship still. They're cheaper than some of the other options so I can make it work even if I don't get a scholarship.

On Sunday, we go to church with my parents and George, but then, Penny and I have plans. First part of it is food. Church is too early and lasts too long to not eat soonafter.

We go to Perkins for breakfast. Penny insists she must sit on Piper's side of the table. From scooting into the side where it looked like she was going initially to eventually crawling under the table to ditch my bench to get to hers. When we order, Piper gets the waffle platter. Penny gets the chocolate chip pancakes with whipped cream and a chocolate milk. I get the Meat 'N Potatoes Omelet. As much as going in public with Penny to somewhere other than church makes me a little bit anxious out of habit, it's nice to take her places and do things. We couldn't really mention Penny out loud in case people heard us. Even when we bought her things at the mall, we checked out the stores first for people we knew and then made sure the stuff we got was in opaque bags.

When the food comes, Penny looks over at Piper's waffles and, seeing all the powdered sugar on top, asks, "I try a bite?"

Penny gives her the puppy dog eyes, so Piper cuts a corner of the waffle off and puts it on her plate. I can't help but laugh. "You can say no, you know."

"No," Penny answers, making us both laugh. She shakes her head vigorously before picking up the fork in her little hand and stabbing the waffle. She nearly misses putting it in her mouth, causing a waterfall of powdered sugar to fall from it and onto her sparkly, black shirt – not that she notices. Her eyes seem to double in size as she chews and bounces up and down in her seat. "This yummy! Yummy, yummy, yummy!" She dances side to side in her seat as she finishes chewing. Nothing like sugar to make my child happy.

Piper barely pauses before trading her waffles for Penny's chocolate chip pancakes.

I give her a doubtful look, trying to ask with my eyes if she actually wanted to trade. In response, Piper just shugs. "They aren't that different." I cut the waffles up while Piper takes her first bite. When she nearly does a happy dance with the sugar mixed with her carbs, I laugh. These two and their sugar obsession really makes them go together well.

Penny manages to finish an entire waffle, meanwhile, dancing and repeating "Yummy!" consistently the entire time that she is eating. At one point, I think if we would've let her out of the booth, she would've run laps around the restaurant or danced in the middle of the floor to let everyone know how good her food was.

When we're all done eating, we get the bill and go to the front to pay. While I pay, Penny admires the muffins for sale. There's a double chocolate chip muffin in there that looks delicious, but both of my girls have already had way too much sugar for their own good.

Getting back to Piper's car, I buckle Penny in to her car seat in the back seat while Piper gets in the front seat and turn the car on to start the heat. As much as switching the car seat sucks, we can't all fit in my truck so it makes a lot more sense to just take Piper's car.

Next stop, the nearest rink, just down the road. There are two different outdoor ice rinks within about a mile of Perkins. If you give us a two-mile radius, the number at least doubles if not triples. In a 20-minute driving radius in our area, I'd be willing to bet there's at least a dozen outdoor skating rinks in addition to at least three indoor rinks for hockey, including the rink our team plays at. Plus, you can always figure in lakes as well, but those aren't as good for little ones like Penny who are still getting the hang of it. Lakes tend to have such bumpy ice.

In the parking lot, I start collecting skates from the car while Piper gets Penny out of the car. By the entrance to the rink, there's a bench we can sit on to change. Being the most practiced at putting skates on, I get mine laced up in about a minute flat and move on to Penny's figure skates. Her practically new skates are finished being laced up about the time Piper finishes with hers. I'm not used to doing figure skates and doing it from another angle messes with me. When I'm done, I plop a pink bike helmet on her head. "Better safe than sorry."

As she stands, she holds tight to my hands, looking terrified at the idea of what she's doing. I hate that I waited until she was this old to get her on skates. "First, we just need to get over to the ice so we're going to walk over there, okay?" I direct. She looks hesitant about this idea, but nods nonetheless. While I step onto the ice, Penny holds onto the boards to keep her balance. "I'm going to pick you up and put you on the ice so you don't have to do it yourself the first time." She nods again. You'd think she doesn't know how to talk with how silent she has suddenly become. Quite the contrast from the kid at Perkins.

I pick her up, but then very slowly set her down on the ice until the blades are holding her up instead of me. I'm not sure she even realizes when it goes from me holding her to her holding herself. She stands as though she's a statue. I move in front of her, taking her hands, and skate backward just a hint so she moves. She lets out a squeak, but lets it happen. As I pull her a little more, she starts to loosen up some, though still not daring to move her feet.

Once we aren't in front of the opening, Piper gets on the ice as well, nearly falling as soon as she steps on. I can't help but laugh. I've seen her skate. This season even. "Do I need to do this with you too?"

She rolls her eyes before taking a few more steps to build a little speed. Quickly, she does a lap of the small rink and makes it back to us. By the time she gets back, Penny has started trying to move her feet as well.

Just as Piper catches up to her, though, Penny's toepick gets caught in the ice and she falls to her knees.

"Go ahead and try to get up. You see daddy fall sometimes when he's playing hockey and I have to get up again and keep skating," I encourage, standing to the side. She lets out some frustrated whines, but she's going to need to know how to get up without someone to help, so I let her do it. Once she's back on her feet, she stands still, expecting me to come back and pull her again. "I want to see you try to skate yourself now."

She sticks out that pouty lip, but it quickly goes away when I shake my head. "You need to try yourself. I can't help you if you don't try on your own." As she looks ahead and takes a couple small steps, I move to Piper, putting my arm around her waist and kissing her forehead. "Thank you for coming with us."

"No problem," she says, just as I hear my name.

We both look towards the parking lot and see a bunch of the guys from the team coming toward us. They're carrying their skates and sticks. "You wanna play, man?" Lev yells. I'm surprised he's conscious before noon on a weekend day.

"Nah, I'm teaching someone how to skate. If you're going to play, can you keep it to half so we don't have to avoid you? She's just figuring out how to stay on her feet, let alone change direction."

"Piper, you don't know how to skate?" Hunter asks. Did none of them notice her skating on the ice that day?

Piper rolls her eyes and shakes her head. "I can skate just fine, thank you very much. I did learn as a kid, just like most Minnesotans."

"Ooooohhhhh," Leo reaches the boards first, leaning against them and checking out what we're doing. "Teaching our little otter?"

"Working on it, at least."

Smiling, Leo says, "Well, you got her the wrong kind of skates. She should be in hockey skates so she can take after you!"

ONE YEAR LATER

I got my eggs, bacon, and a bowl of cereal, Penny got coffee cake and a bowl of cereal. I drop the food at the table. First ones here. Penny, in her jeans and Yellowjackets sweatshirt, climbs up into her chair while I go get us something to drink. By the time I get back with milk for our cereal, chocolate milk for Penny, and orange juice for me, Penny is practically surrounded. Piper is right next to her, but more of the team has arrived. My girls have taken to sitting at the table with the rest of the team.

"Hey, Penny, who's going to score today?" James asks. Penny points to him and then looks around to find me, pointing to me. She always picks me, but she's gotten used to me not scoring every game anymore. College is definitely tougher, but I like the challenge. No injuries yet, thankfully.

"Hey, baby girl," I say, kissing her on the forehead before collapsing into the chair next to her. I pour milk into her bowl, and some into mine, leaving just a little bit left in the bottom of the cup.

"Hi, Daddy," she answers, smiling up at me. Sitting on her knees, she picks up her fork to take a bite of the coffee cake.

"Are you going to watch with Piper today?"

"Hmmmm," she answers, looking like she's thinking. When she looks over to Piper, she starts giggling. "Maybe I stand by glass?"

"You can for a little bit, but you don't want to block other people's views. Other people want to see the boys play too," Piper explains.

Looking around at the other boys sitting at the table now, Penny wrinkles her nose and says, "Noooooo." She zeroes in on James straight across from her and drinks the last couple of sips of milk. Sitting up to be as tall as she can, kneeling on the chair, she leans across the table and puts her now empty cup in James's cup. It's a game the team plays and has taught Penny. You want to stack your cup on someone else's empty cup and don't want to be the one left with the huge stack.

I've learned the hard way not to totally empty our milk cup. Not only do the boys start stacking it, but then Penny doesn't get to stack other people. She can't stack other people as easily with multiple cups, so instead, we save the cup until she finds someone she can get. Maybe it's a good thing to expose her to more people, but maybe I don't need to expose her to all these college antics when she's only in preschool.

ACKNOWLEDGMENTS

I can't fully believe I'm actually putting a book full of my writing out into the world. This book has been about 6 years in slow progress since I started it around COVID. It was written between shifts at the hospital (and some nights, even at the nurse's station). It started fully in Piper's point of view, and made a huge shift. Through all it's iterations, though, I've loved this story and wanted to put it into the world in the hopes at least one person would love it as much as I do.

Thank you to Christine Cover Design on Etsy who made my beautiful cover.

Thank you to Sarah, Kim, and my amazing mom who all read this at various points whether to help find the story and things we needed more of or simply finding grammatical errors. And to Kory for answering my questions having to do with the scouting process. Any errors in the hockey/scouting parts is my own error.

Thank you to all my friends who hyped up my writing, the idea of self-publishing, and my cover, plus any extra encouragement I needed in the process to keep me working on it instead of just sticking it back in the drafts.

Thank you to my daughter for simply existing and being the sweetest and later being an adorable little inspiration, even if most of this book was written before you were ever born, and some days you're more of a distraction than anything from things that involve sitting down.

Finally, an extra big thank you to my amazing husband for helping get things done around the house so I could work on this book. Thank you for being the first to read it. Thank you for showing me what a loving partner is and helping me live our own love story. You will forever be my book boyfriend inspiration.